What Others Are Saying
about R.J. Patterson

"R.J. Patterson does a fantastic job at keeping you engaged and interested. I look forward to more from this talented author."

- Aaron Patterson
bestselling author of SWEET DREAMS

DEAD SHOT

"Small town life in southern Idaho might seem quaint and idyllic to some. But when local newspaper reporter Cal Murphy begins to uncover a series of strange deaths that are linked to a sticky spider web of deception, the lid on the peaceful town is blown wide open. Told with all the energy and bravado of an old pro, first-timer R.J. Patterson hits one out of the park his first time at bat with *Dead Shot*. It's that good."

- Vincent Zandri
bestselling author of THE REMAINS

"You can tell R.J. knows what it's like to live in the newspaper world, but with *Dead Shot*, he's proven that he also can write one heck of a murder mystery."

- Josh Katzowitz
NFL writer for CBSSports.com
& author of Sid Gillman: Father of the Passing Game

"Patterson has a mean streak about a mile wide and puts his two main characters through quite a horrible ride, which makes for good reading."

- Richard D., reader

DEAD LINE

"This book kept me on the edge of my seat the whole time. I didn't really want to put it down. R.J. Patterson has hooked me. I'll be back for more."

- Bob Behler
3-time Idaho broadcaster of the year
and play-by-play voice for Boise State football

"Like a John Grisham novel, from the very start I was pulled right into the story and couldn't put the book down. It was as if I personally knew and cared about what happened to each of the main characters. Every chapter ended with so much excitement and suspense I had to continue to read until I learned how it ended, even though it kept me up until 3:00 A.M.

- Ray F., reader

DEAD IN THE WATER

"In Dead in the Water, R.J. Patterson accurately captures the action-packed saga of a what could be a real-life college football scandal. The sordid details will leave readers flipping through the pages as fast as a hurry-up offense."

- Mark Schlabach,
ESPN college sports columnist and
co-author of *Called to Coach*
and *Heisman: The Man Behind the Trophy*

THE WARREN OMISSIONS

"What can be more fascinating than a super high concept novel that reopens the conspiracy behind the JFK assassination while the threat of a global world war rests in the balance? With his new novel, *The Warren Omissions*, former journalist turned bestselling author R.J. Patterson proves he just might be the next worthy successor to Vince Flynn."

- Vincent Zandri
bestselling author of THE REMAINS

CODE
RED

A Brady Hawk novel

R.J.
PATTERSON

For Earle, a good friend
and a great American

CHAPTER 1

Chagai Hills, Pakistan

BRADY HAWK'S JEEP RUMBLED across the rocky road leading to the Rico Dig mines as he inhaled the fresh air. The patches of snow still clinging to existence along the mountainous terrain reflected the afternoon sunshine, glints of bright light temporarily blinding Hawk as he sped along. Even in the midst of a place as forsaken as this, he found moments to appreciate the natural beauty surrounding him. A mile from his position, black smoke chugged into the air, a fitting cover for an Al Fatihin hideout.

"How's our connection?" Hawk asked Alex. She was stationed in the Phoenix Foundation's offices in Washington.

"I hear you loud and clear," Alex said. "Ready for another day of mayhem?"

"Some people might call it mayhem, but it's just another Wednesday for me."

She chuckled. "Always so cool under fire."

"The fire hasn't started yet, but I'm expecting it to come at me fast and fierce when they figure out what I'm doing."

What Hawk was doing was ignoring several treaties in his covert mission, all under the direction of President Noah Young. With his approval ratings dropping and Al Fatihin leader Evana Bahar exposing his dealings with terrorists to the nation, Young needed something to unify the American people, if even for a day. He wanted them to forget about all the dividing partisan politics and celebrate the homecoming of a hero. And for Young, it would also mean the homecoming of a friend, former Navy SEAL and CIA operative Frank Stone.

The stress of leading a country mired in constant bickering over political issues had taken its toll on Young. Instead of leading from a position of strength, he found himself holding his finger up to see which way the majority winds were blowing. The result was a meandering direction along with an accompanying health issue that required him to have a pacemaker put in, something only a handful of people knew about. If only for twenty-four hours, he needed a respite and the press to talk about something else other than idle speculation and scurrilous accusations against his administration. And Hawk was the man chosen to make everything happen.

Hawk tapped the steering wheel as he rode along, singing Led Zeppelin's Kashmir. He was close enough to the disputed region he figured that it was an appropriate time as any to belt out the lyrics.

"You do realize that I can hear you, right?" Alex said.

Hawk resisted answering her since he was in the middle of the chorus.

"Hawk? Are your coms still working? You need to answer me and confirm."

Hawk sighed. "Alex, you're ruining my moment here. I'm about to spend the next hour fighting Al Fatihin goons. All I want is a little moment to relax and clear my head with some of the greatest music from the 70s."

"You weren't even alive in the 70s."

"I know I missed it by a few years, but when it comes to music, that's my decade. Now, can you let me finish my song in peace?"

"I'd love to, but I'm watching the satellite images here and just noticed something that I thought you needed to know."

Hawk groaned. "What is it now?"

"I see a pair of Jeeps about two miles behind you," Alex said. "And as far as I can tell, they have machine guns mounted on the roll bars."

"Pakistan is such a welcoming country. You know, it's moments like these that I wish I had a drone so I could fire missiles at those thugs to keep them off my tail."

"Well, this isn't James Bond. You have to do things the old fashioned way. Now, just make sure you hide your vehicle. The CIA evac team is fueling up just across the border in Afghanistan. They'll be awaiting my word, so make sure you stay in touch."

"Roger that," Hawk said before he resumed his song.

When he finished, he slowed down as he approached the gates of the mining site. The Chinese and the Pakistanis struck a deal to develop the mine and process the resources found there. And with a high daily yield, both countries worked hard to protect their investment with stringent security measures.

Hawk held out his papers for the guard as he approached the vehicle. He studied the papers for a moment before handing them back and waving Hawk inside.

With the operation to retrieve Frank Stone a collaborative effort between the Phoenix Foundation and the CIA, Hawk had access to more resources than ever. The CIA created a low-key legend for him as a geologist studying copper mines around the world. They even hired someone to write a book about copper mining and stuck Hawk's picture on the back to further legitimize his standing as an authority in his field. Instead of keeping his fingers crossed that he wouldn't meet any resistance in Pakistan, he was welcomed as a celebrity among the engineers partnering on the mine with the Chinese and Pakistanis. And a week before Hawk arrived, nobody would've even been able to find his existence on the web.

"I found the perfect spot for you," Alex said. "Just head east, and there's a nook at the base of the mountain you should be able to squeeze your Jeep into."

"Heading that way now," Hawk said.

A couple of minutes later, he came to the location Alex suggested and parked. Using his access badge, he swiped it across a security scanner adjacent to a door built into the wall. Once the locked clicked free, he entered the structure and began his search for Al Fatihin's hideout.

"All right, Alex," Hawk said. "I'm in. Keep me on the right path, okay?"

"I'm overlaying your position now with the schematics of the mine," she said. "We've got the NSA to thank for hacking those Chinese computers and pulling up the plans for this facility."

"Stop brownnosing. You know the NSA is

listening to this conversation. You're just trying to get on their good side in case you ever get—"

"That's enough, Hawk. Not everything I've done is documented, even by the NSA."

Hawk chuckled. "I going into the stairwell now."

He hustled down the steps, emerging on a floor three levels below where he started. If the Chinese were anything, they were concerned with safety in their construction of the mine, which ran contrary to everything Hawk had heard about projects of this magnitude in China. There were escape hatches and stairways everywhere he looked, making the fringe portion of the mine seem more like a vast maze than a place that was digging up copper and gold at an astounding rate.

As Hawk crept down the hallway, he whispered into his coms. "Do you have a location for Stone now?"

"I have a guess," Alex offered.

"A guess? You do realize this isn't the kind of place where I need to be speculating, don't you?"

"There are four potential areas where Al Fatihin's hideout could be located. And if prior intel on Chinese construction procedures is accurate, one of those spots belongs to the mine's labor offices."

"And the other three?"

"I'd be playing a hunch if I told you."

Hawk sighed. "Might as well hear it at this point."

"I was hoping you'd say that," Alex said. "So, while studying the schematics, conventional wisdom would tell you that if you were wanting to hide something, you'd put it deeper into the ground. However, when comparing this with other mines built by this same Chinese corporation, I found that they usually put a survival room near the initial bottom floor of the mine in case something happens. It gives the workers a place to retreat to as well as a chance at survival if there is a collapse."

"Get to the part where you tell me which one it is, Alex."

"There's a survival room on the fourth floor that has two tunnels leading to the surface, neither of which are visible from the outside. I'm guessing those are secret entrances."

"And why would you make an escape route hidden to the outside?"

"Exactly," Alex said. "Try the one on the south side of the fourth floor."

"Roger that."

Hawk hustled along the inside wall. The hallway was devoid of any workers as the resources on the level had apparently been long since exhausted. When he reached the room, he stopped and stared at the lock, which was comprised of a numerical pad and a spot for a fingerprint.

"Alex, got any ideas about how I can crack a keypad that requires a touch identification?" Hawk asked in a hushed tone.

"Short of severing someone's thumb, no," she said. "At least, not at this juncture in the operation. Had I known this earlier—"

"I know," Hawk said. "You would've had all your bases covered. But this intel came along so fast and out of nowhere that the higher ups didn't want to delay for fear that Stone might be moved again."

"Well, you're there now," she said. "My best advice would be to camp out down the hall and wait for someone to exit the room. Then hope you can grab the door before it locks shut."

"That's not what I wanted to hear. I was hoping you might at least figure out a way to unlock the door or something more useful than telling me to stakeout the entrance to Al Fatihin, especially when I have no idea what awaits me on the other side."

"Sorry to disappoint you, honey. I'm sure you'll do fine. Just keep me posted."

"Roger that," he said before he retreated down the hallway and took up a position around the corner, just out of the line of sight from anyone exiting the room. His minutes were marked by glances down one side and peeks around the other.

"Do I still have company outside?" Hawk asked Alex after a few minutes.

"You know, that's the strangest thing," she said. "They drove up to your Jeep and after a few minutes just drove off, heading back where they came from."

"Do you think they tried to sabotage it with a bomb?"

"I didn't see anyone get inside or slide underneath the car."

"Weird."

An hour went by without any activity.

"Hawk," Alex said, "you still awake?"

"Vigilant as ever. I'm beginning to wonder if this place isn't a front for some other activity. I don't even hear a light bulb humming overhead."

"Just give it some time. Someone will come out of there eventually."

"That's what I'm afraid of," Hawk said. "Because eventually I'll be asleep. This kind of assignment is exactly why I didn't become a detective."

"And being a sniper is so much different? You're hunkered down prone in a blind just waiting for someone to move."

"Far more exciting than sitting in a car or slumped against the wall in a hallway."

Alex said something else, but Hawk had already tuned her out. A faint click in the direction of the door arrested his attention. Hawk crept closer to the corner and sat on his haunches as he waited for someone to poke their head outside. After a few seconds, a man lumbered through the exit and turned in the opposite direction of Hawk. Once his back was fully to the door, Hawk stealthily hustled up to it and wedged his foot inside. In a deft move, he slithered inside and let the door shut naturally. Without having to invoke a confrontation, Hawk could slip inside more easily. However, it also meant the man's return would remain a mystery until Hawk escaped with Stone.

Hawk stopped and read a verse the Quran painted in Arabic on the entryway wall. The translation amounted to roughly this in English: "And slay them wherever ye find them, and drive them out of the places whence they drove you out, for persecution is worse than slaughter . . . and fight them until fitnah is no more, and religion is for Allah."

After spending so much time in Afghanistan with the Peace Corps, Hawk was all too familiar with Quran 2:191. The passage always evoked a shiver, fearing that one day more Muslims than not might take that ancient scripture to heart. Peace was challenging to achieve in the Middle East when only a small portion of the Muslim community took those words literally. The moment that the majority of followers of Islam started to believe that was a command instead of just a suggestion, the world would fall into chaos.

Not surprised to see that verse here.

Hawk never looked at his role as an operative working in the Middle East as someone who was fighting against Islam. For him, the work was always about stopping terrorists bound and determined to visit harm on innocent people, whether they were American or any other nationality. And he enjoyed it, perhaps a little more than he should have.

"Found it," Hawk said in a whisper over his coms.

"Roger that," Alex said. "Just give me the word when you've secured Stone so I can send in the evac team. They're on standby."

Hawk checked his gun before continuing on. He tightened the silencer and removed the safety. As he forged ahead, he cleared each room and hallway, finding them empty with minimal furniture. The doors were made out of opaque glass, forcing Hawk to check each one. Still no signs of life other than the man who initially exited into the hallway.

When Hawk reached the end of the corridor, he only had one door remaining. Easing inside, he found a man sitting on a couch with his back to the entrance while watching television. He broke into laughter at the sitcom dubbed in Arabic. Hawk didn't recognize the show, but he could tell the man was part of Al

Fatihin. Unable to determine if anyone else was nearby, Hawk went ahead and put a bullet in the back of the man's head as he was guffawing over the latest funny one liner.

Can't be the worst way to go.

Hawk noticed a door just on the other side of the television. When he went inside, he found it starkly different than the comfortable confines the guard enjoyed. There was no plush chair or warm light. Instead, the prison cell was comprised of a cot on the concrete floor, a bucket to do his business in, and a pale fluorescent bulb that flickered every few seconds. And sitting with his back against the wall was Frank Stone.

His shirt was tattered, stained with a mixture of blood and dirt. With a scraggly beard and unkempt hair, Stone looked like he hadn't showered since Al Fatihin captured him six months earlier.

"Well, I wouldn't believe it unless I saw it with my own eyes," Stone said.

"Gotta move now," Hawk said. "There'll be plenty of time for you to gush about your surprise."

Stone didn't move, instead grinning and pointing at Hawk. "Noah put you up to this, didn't he?"

"We really need to go right now."

"Who are you? CIA? Navy SEALs? Army Rangers?"

"I'm Hawk, and this isn't a game, Lieutenant Colonel. But I think you know that."

Stone shook his head. "You're right. It's not. But if there aren't more of you, we're screwed."

"How come?"

"There are a dozen men who watch this facility twenty-four seven," Stone said.

"There are only eleven now."

Hawk led Stone into the adjacent room and pointed at the dead guard.

Stone grabbed Hawk by the arm. "I'm serious. There are plenty more men roaming the halls of this place with guns. They're not going to ask questions. They're just going to shoot."

Hawk grinned wryly. "That's exactly what I'm hoping for."

He knelt down and removed his pack from his back.

"What are you doing?" Stone asked. "We don't have time for this. Someone is going to be in here any minute now."

Hawk tossed a hard hat at Stone along with a pair of coveralls, matching that of the mine employees.

"What's this for?" Stone asked.

"That's your plan B in case we get separated. There's going to be a chopper waiting for us at an extraction point on the north side of the mountain in about half an hour from now."

"I'd rather have a gun."

Hawk dug through his bag and retrieved another weapon. "I figured you might. Now put on that uniform so we can get going."

While Stone got dressed, Hawk alerted Alex that it was time to send the helicopter. Then the two men ventured into the main corridor of the Al Fatihin hideout.

"So you've tried to escape before?" Hawk whispered.

"Several times, but this place is like a maze—and it's heavily guarded."

"So where is everyone today?"

Stone shrugged. "Beats me. But I wouldn't be so sure that you've entered at just the right time."

They crept along without incident until they reached the exit.

"You ready?" Hawk asked.

Stone nodded.

Crouching low, Hawk went first and checked in both directions. With the coast clear, he signaled for Stone to join him. They moved stealthily toward the corner and peered around it. Hawk noticed two guards walking toward him.

"We've got two hostiles heading our way," Hawk said. "I take the one on the right; you take the one on the left."

"Roger that," Stone said.

"On my mark."

When Hawk gave the order, both men swung out around the corner and hit the unsuspecting men before they had a chance to fire back. Hawk and Stone stripped the guards of their guns and checked to make sure they were dead.

"That's funny," Stone said. "I don't recognize either of these guys."

"Are they not Al Faithin?"

Stone slid one of the men's right sleeve down his arm and held it up for Hawk to see. Etched into his wrist was a tattoo with the words "Al Fatihin" written in Arabic and a shamshir.

"We got the right guys, but I've never seen them before."

"Is that unusual?"

"I knew most of the Al Fatihin operatives by name. It was always the same group of men—and sometimes the woman."

"Evana Bahar?"

Stone nodded.

"Let's keep moving," Hawk said.

They navigated toward the stairwell, where they found another lone Al Fatihin agent. Hawk shot the man in the chest at point-blank range before he could react.

"The chopper is two minutes out, Hawk," Alex said over the coms.

"We're almost there," he said. "Are we still clean outside?"

"Clean as a whistle."

Hawk and Stone hustled up to ground level and exited on the north side of the mountain where the CIA helicopter was stirring up a small dust storm. Glancing back one final time to make sure there were no Al Fatihin soldiers behind them, Hawk gestured for Stone to run. Hawk followed suit, jogging backward with his gun trained on the door in case any agents spilled outside.

Once Hawk and Stone were safely inside, the pilot took off and peeled away from the mountains to safety across the border in Afghanistan.

"As far as ops go, that was rather uneventful," Stone said.

"Too uneventful," Hawk said. "Something doesn't seem right."

"Are you clear now?" Alex asked.

"We're clear," Hawk said. "Get the message to the president that we've got Stone."

Hawk patted Stone on the back. "Rest up. You've got a long journey ahead of you, and a lot of people want to talk to you."

CHAPTER 2

Puyuhuapi, Chile

TITUS BLACK INHALED the fresh mountain air and slung his pack across his shoulders. He checked his weapon to make sure it was loaded before beginning the long climb up the gravel road. To his back was a stunning view of the Puyuhuapi fjord where the sun glistened off the turquoise water.

Not a bad place to hide.

With Hawk dispatched to fulfill President Young's request to extract an American agent right from underneath the noses of Al Fatihin, General Van Fortner was still on the lam following the shooting at the National Security Complex in Langley. The Phoenix Foundation head J.D. Blunt ignored Young's pleas to concentrate all of the organization's resources on bringing home the CIA operative. According to Blunt, Fortner was the new key to unlocking the mystery of Obsidian and finding a way to infiltrate the group of people pulling the strings, particularly learning more about the fastest-growing social media platform in the world, Sermo, and its Russian billionaire owner Tanya Starikov.

It had taken nearly six weeks to get a potential location for Fortner, but when Blunt received one, he immediately dispatched Black to take care of the general.

The road up to Fortner's hideout was steep, resulting in a leg burn even for someone in as good of shape as Black. A light fog drifted over the chaquiro pines and Andean oaks covering the mountainside, providing an ethereal feel to the hike. Patagonian sierra finches chirped their morning melodies, providing a peaceful soundtrack, which Black found to be an odd prelude to what was sure to be a violent confrontation.

After a half hour, Black crested a hill and reached a small terrace. A small wooden cabin was situated on the far side of the property next to a pond fed by a stream trickling down the mountain. As the sun fought through the dispersing clouds, Black noticed a man fishing from the dock.

In an effort to maintain the element of surprise, Black ducked into the woods. He was astonished to find Fortner living so freely, devoid of any armed protection. Surely he could've afforded such a necessity. But from Black's initial survey of the area, Fortner lived simply—and lived alone.

A small bush hog and a tractor were scattered across the property along with bales of hay and a fenced in pasture for a horse. Instead of working his way from object to object in search of cover, Black retreated into the forest encircling Fortner's land.

Black eased into a position where he had a clear shot. Confident that there was no way the general could work the situation to his advantage, Black walked out into the open with his weapon trained on Fortner.

"Keep your hands where I can see them," Black said.

Fortner chuckled and continued clutching his fishing rod. "I hope you can see what I'm holding onto here. It's certainly not a weapon, but I've actually got my first bite of the day."

"Drop it," Black said.

Fortner remained defiant. "If you want to shoot me, go ahead. I couldn't stop you if I wanted to, but I wouldn't advise that."

"Of course you wouldn't, General. We all know you do whatever it takes to save your own hide or fatten your pocket, whatever the case may be."

Fortner looked over his shoulder and sneered. "You don't know anything."

"I'm going to shoot it out of your hand if you don't put the rod down on the dock now."

Fortner sighed and finally obliged. The pole didn't move.

"Must've been one helluva fish," Black said. "It couldn't even drag your rod into the water."

"I didn't say it was a keeper," Fortner said, raising his hands and turning around slowly to face Black. "So, what took you so long? I figured you would've found me weeks ago."

"Sorry to damage your ego like that, but we have bigger fish to fry," Black said.

"What do you want from me? Because if you wanted me dead, I imagine I would already be floating in that pond right now."

"I want you to come with me," Black said. "You need to answer for what you did, for your treasonous acts, for your unwillingness to stop a hostile force attempting to infiltrate our government. That enough for you?"

Fortner shrugged. "Maybe, but I'm not going anywhere."

Black steadied his hand on his gun. "General, that's not a wise decision. I've been authorized to take you out if necessary."

"So, I'm already seen as expendable?" Fortner asked before taking a deep breath and then exhaling slowly. "That's not a way to encourage me to work with you."

"I was hoping I wouldn't have to persuade you with physical force."

Fortner paced along the dock, his hands still raised in the air. "It'd be a shame for you to resort to such action, at least it'd be a shame for your sister."

Black narrowed his eyes. "My sister?"

Fortner held up one hand while he eased the other toward his pocket. "Don't get jumpy. I'm just reaching for my phone. There's something you need to see."

Fortner produced his cell and held it out gingerly to Black.

"What's this?" he asked.

"Have a look for yourself," Fortner said. "I'm sure you're smart enough to figure it out."

Black grabbed the phone before backing away. He glanced between the screen and Fortner, trying to discern the nature of the image on the screen. The picture was so still that Black was convinced it was just a photo. That is until the woman lying on the bed moved. She rolled over, and Black immediately recognized his sister's face.

He glared at Fortner. "You took Laura? You sonofabitch, I ought to shoot you right now. You know she's got nothing to do with any of this."

"Of course I do," Fortner said. "But this is how you play the game if you want to stay in it. I could tell you why I'm doing what I'm doing, but you won't believe me, so I have to resort to other methods to maintain the upper hand. Unfortunately, your sister is just collateral."

"Her name is Laura," Black said with a growl. "Laura. Say it with me."

"I'm well aware of her name."

"Then say it!"

Fortner ignored the demand. "You've said it enough for the both of us. I'm not interested in playing your mind games where you try to humanize everyone. I've been through the same training you have, probably more. And it's not going to make any difference if I say Laura out loud or not."

"What do you want?" Black asked.

"I want you to lower your weapon. Let's talk about your future."

"I want to talk about you letting Laura go."

Fortner nodded. "Perhaps we will, but in the meantime we have more pertinent matters to discuss, like you joining forces with Obsidian."

Black chuckled and shook his head. "I thought you knew what kind of man I am, General. If you did, you'd certainly know I'm not the kind to betray my country."

"I'm not asking you to betray your country. I'm simply extending an invitation for you to be on the ground floor of a world takeover that will leave you on the outside if you don't get in now. Laura is simply my way of ensuring you choose wisely. So how do you want this to play out?"

"Doesn't sound like I have much of a choice," Black said.

"You don't," Fortner said. "But I'll give you twenty-four hours to consider it. I'll ring you tomorrow morning at the village hotel, which is where I assume you're staying. You can let me know your decision then. And it should go without saying, but don't tell a soul."

Black flung the phone back at Fortner, hitting him in the chest. He pocketed the device and picked up his fishing rod off the dock.

Black walked backward, clutching his lowered weapon. While mustering all the restraint he could, he refrained from filling Fortner with lead.

* * *

WHEN BLACK RETURNED to the hotel, he received a call from Blunt inquiring if the operation had gone smoothly.

"Do you have Fortner?" Blunt asked.

"It was a dead end," Black said. "Must've been some bad intel."

"Damn it," Blunt said. "Fortner needs to answer for what he's done. We're still groping in the dark when it comes to Obsidian. We need him."

"I know. You have no idea how disappointed I am."

"When are you coming back?"

Black sighed. "I already missed the morning plane out of here for Santiago, so it'll be tomorrow that I'll begin the journey home, unless you can send your plane."

"Hawk and Alex have it. Just keep me updated if anything changes or someone in the village talks."

"Roger that," Black said before he hung up.

He slammed his fist into the bed and let out a scream. Black hated lying almost as much as he hated being coopted into helping the enemy.

And he had no choice but to do both.

CHAPTER 3

Tangier, Morocco

FRANK STONE DABBED his face with a towel before settling onto a small bench just outside the showers. When he finished, he was in the middle of pulling on a pair of boxers when he looked up and jumped.

"What's wrong with you people?" Stone asked. "Can't I get just a moment of peace and get dressed before you start interviewing me?"

Hawk shook his head. "I wish I could, but time is of the essence. And I swear you took an hour in there."

"I could've stayed in longer. You have no idea what filthy is until you've been captured by those animals."

"Unfortunately, I'm all too familiar with what that's like."

"What a minute," Stone said, pointing his index

finger at Hawk, "are you the guy who took out Karif Fazil?"

"Guilty as charged. And a lot of good that did. The newest iteration of Al Hasib has returned with a vengeance."

"And some unlikely bedfellows."

Hawk's eyebrows shot upward. "This sounds interesting."

"I'll tell you all about it after I get dressed. Now, do you mind?"

Hawk sighed. "Five minutes. Your buddy Randy Wood from the CIA is here. He's less patient than any of us."

"Five minutes, I promise."

* * *

HAWK SETTLED INTO his chair at the table and informed the rest of the people in attendance that Stone would be out momentarily. Joining Hawk for the interview was Wood, who was the deputy director of the CIA, along with Martina Bingham, the CIA's station chief for the Middle East. Alex and Blunt were listening in via speakerphone on a secure line.

"Stone was teasing me with some information, so I'm hoping we get something good out of this," Hawk said.

"Me too," Martina said as she tucked her straight brown hair behind her ears.

Wood was slouched in his chair, chewing on a pen and finger combing his graying mop of a hairdo. "I wish he'd hurry up. We seriously need to get moving on this. Every minute we wait—"

"Randy," Stone said as he entered the room. "I bet you couldn't wait for me to get here."

"I couldn't, but not for the reasons you think. What were you thinking getting yourself in that situation with Al Fatihin? We warned you that such brazen behavior was going to expose you. Fortunately, we escaped your debacle without the loss of any assets."

Stone settled into a seat directly across the table from Wood. "I also escaped with some amazing intel that should help us capture Evana Bahar and put an end to this terrorist organization once and for all."

"Frank, are you okay?" Martina asked. "You don't have to do this right now if you need some more time."

Wood shot a glance at Martina. "Are you crazy? We absolutely need him to share this information with us right now."

"Sorry for trying to be—I don't know—a human," she said.

Hawk leaned forward in his chair and eyed Stone. "Why don't you proceed?"

"I'm fine, Martina, and I hope Brooke and the children are too," Stone began.

She nodded. "Everyone's good and looking forward to seeing you when you get back on U.S. soil."

"Which is never going to happen if we continue at this pace," Wood said, slamming his pen on the table. "Evana Bahar may very well rule the world by the time we find out this big secret that you have."

Stone sighed. "Fine. I'll tell you what I know."

"That'd be refreshing," said Wood, scooting up in his chair before sliding a notebook in front of Stone.

"So, there's a lot to unpack from my time both infiltrating the organization as well as my time in captivity," Stone said. "But I'll skip to the most important part first: Evana Bahar is heading to Istanbul tomorrow to meet with Russian arms dealer, Andrei Orlovsky."

Wood cocked his head to one side and furrowed his brow. "How do you know this?"

"Because I heard them talking about it two days ago," Stone said.

"You heardthem? Who talks about plans in front of a prisoner?" Wood asked, eyeing Stone carefully.

"Just in case you've forgotten, I was being detained in a hideout located in a mine," Stone said. "And if you know anything about mines, it's that they are very well ventilated. I assure you I could hear everything as if I were sitting in the same room with them."

"And you're sure you heard them discussing these plans?" Martina asked.

"Yes."

"And was this a regular occurrence?" Wood asked.

"Whenever Evana Bahar was there, I regularly heard them discussing plans for different operations, though I could only recall a few of them. I heard her talking about going to Cuba once. Did that happen?"

Hawk nodded. "She tried to take out the president. But we stopped her."

"Yet she got away," Wood said. "Otherwise, we might not be having this conversation."

"Well, you can save the commentary," Hawk said. "However, if that's the kind of things Stone was hearing then it's difficult to doubt the veracity of his claim."

"I've been following her long before she was a running Al Fatihin," Martina said. "The agency was watching her when she was in London with her nonprofit and she fought in a few skirmishes in Kandahar under another alias. She's very ambitious, and she probably feels like she's waited long enough to make a statement."

Wood nodded in agreement and looked at Hawk. "Based on some of the wiretaps we've heard, she wants you dead more than anything. She's still smarting about you killing her cousin."

"She'll be next if she keeps this up. Then she can go join Karif Fazil."

Blunt cleared his throat, interrupting the conversation as his voice boomed over the speaker. "This is all interesting, but that doesn't change the fact that we need to do something with this intel. Is it actionable? That's what we need to be asking ourselves."

"If Evana Bahar is going to Istanbul to meet with Orlovsky, we definitely need to do something about it," Wood said. "This isn't the kind of thing we can sit back on, especially if we can capture or eliminate two high-value targets at once."

"I recommend we go after them," Martina said.

"That's like trying to find a needle in a haystack at this point," Alex said. "Orlovsky is incredibly cautious, and if we don't have any intel on where they're going to meet, we're going to come up empty."

"Then what do you suggest we do?" Wood asked. "Just sit back and do nothing while Evana Bahar plots her revenge on the world and takes another shot at the president?"

"We can prevent the meeting from ever happening," Blunt said. "I can call in a few favors and have the Turkish border agents be on the lookout for her."

"And what? Just tell us that they found her?" Wood asked.

Blunt grunted. "If I ask nicely—something you know nothing about, Randy—they will detain her at the border."

"Sounds like a reasonable compromise," Martina said. "If we get Evana, at least we've prevented something that Al Fatihin could've done. And based on her track record, it'd likely be something devastating."

"I'll place a few calls," Blunt said before he hung up.

* * *

BLUNT THUMBED THROUGH his contact list until he found Omer Demir's number. When Blunt was serving in the senate, he met Demir once during a special Security Council envoy to Europe and the Middle East. The two connected over Demir's love for baseball and the fact that Nolan Ryan was his all-time favorite baseball player. That sealed the friendship for Blunt, which prompted him to send Demir a ball signed by the Hall of Fame pitcher.

"Think he can really help?" Alex asked.

"We're about to find out."

Blunt dialed Demir's number. He picked up after the phone rang twice.

"J.D. Blunt," Demir said, "to what do I owe the pleasure of this call? It's been a long time."

"Far too long, my friend," Blunt said. "How's your family?"

"Getting bigger all the time. I have three grandchildren now."

"Spoiling them rotten, I'm sure."

"Of course," Demir said. "Now, I doubt you just called me up out of the blue to talk about my family, so how can I help you?"

"Well, I believe I need some help detaining someone who is very much wanted for terrorism against our country."

"I hope you have a name," Demir said. "Those people seem to be pouring into our country by the dozens each day."

"I'll do even better than that," Blunt said. "I'll send you a picture you can upload to your database and search through facial recognition."

"That would be helpful. And when do you expect this person to arrive in Turkey?"

"Sometime this week."

"What is this man's name?" Demir asked.

"Actually, it's a woman. Maybe you've heard of her? Evana Bahar?"

"Evana Bahar is coming here?"

"It'd be a major coup if you can arrest her. And you'd win praise from the security community the world over if you snatch Andrei Orlovsky, too."

"That's who she's meeting here?"

"From what we understand, they're scheduled to

talk sometime this week in Istanbul," Blunt said. "It'd be nice to wait until they're meeting together to grab them, but that'd be kind of risky. You know the saying, a bird in the hand is worth two in the bush?"

"We don't say that here in Turkey, but I know what it means. We have another saying that is appropriate for this situation—a city you can see in the distance doesn't require a guide."

Blunt stroked his chin. "In other words, we know where this is headed?"

"Precisely. Stopping them from meeting is of utmost importance. If we arrest both of them, their underlings will continue the business dealings, but if they never meet . . ."

"I'm sending you the photo right now. Upload it to your database, and call me back whenever you get a hit."

"Of course. And it was good to speak with you as always, J.D.," Demir said before ending the call.

Blunt lumbered down the hall. He told Alex to pack her bags to get ready to go to Istanbul.

"She's already been arrested?" she asked.

"Not yet, but I want you to be there to interrogate her the minute she is. Get to the airport. Wheels up in an hour."

He meandered back to his office and then collapsed into his chair. After blowing out a long breath, he leaned back and gazed outside at the city's twinkling lights. He'd come in far too early for the conference call to hear the initial interview with Frank Stone and realized a cup of coffee or three was necessary to make it through the day. Yet Blunt didn't have the energy to go to the break room and make a pot.

While he intended to use the extra time to catch up on some paperwork, he propped his feet up on his desk and fell asleep in a matter of minutes. The ring of his phone startled him awake a half hour later.

"This is Blunt," he said, trying to sound as if he'd been awake for hours.

"We have her," the man said.

Blunt was still groggy, and it took him a few seconds to recognize Demir's voice. "Her?"

"Evana Bahar," Demir said. "We got a hit at the customs office in the Istanbul airport fifteen minutes after we loaded her picture into the system."

"I've got agents on the way. How long can you keep her there?"

"Well, there's more to it than that."

"Oh," Blunt said. "Did you catch Andrei Orlovsky too?"

"That would've been nice, but there's a problem with your Evana Bahar. We did a quick DNA test just to make sure it was her, comparing the sample against what's in the Interpol database that Scotland Yard collected when she was in London."

"And?"

"It's not a match."

"What do you mean?"

"This woman is nearly a perfect facial match for Evana Bahar but isn't who she appears to be."

CHAPTER 4

Istanbul, Turkey

HAWK WAS GRATEFUL for the opportunity to work in the field with Alex, especially on such a case as fascinating as the one given to them. The Phoenix Foundation had hoped that running the errand of extracting someone for the president wouldn't be in vain. And based on the intel gleaned from the first meeting with Frank Stone, the assignment proved to be incredibly valuable. However, Hawk was starting to wonder if Al Fatihin had a deeper agenda at play.

Hawk hugged Alex when they met outside the customs office. Omer Demir greeted them and ushered them inside for a short debriefing.

"Have a seat," Demir said, gesturing for them to sit across the desk from him. "Now, as you already know, that woman is not Evana Bahar. We haven't done any further questioning of her because we have no reason to. However, out of courtesy to my friend

J.D. Blunt, I asked that she be detained for two more hours from now at which time she'll be released. My only request is that once you are finished questioning her, you leave her alone. I don't want an international incident on my hands."

"What's her name?" Alex asked.

"Her passport says Jahedah Khan. But I'm not sure if any of that is authentic."

"You have our word," Hawk said. "Blunt speaks highly of you, and we fully intend to respect your conditions."

Demir stood and then walked around his desk toward the door. "Since we have settled that matter, follow me. I'll take you to her."

Hawk and Alex scurried after Demir, who strode swiftly down the hall. When he reached an interrogation room, he unlocked the door and held it open for Hawk and Alex.

"If you need anything, there is an office next to yours that will be able to assist you in whatever manner you require," Demir said. "I hope you find what you're looking for."

Hawk shot a quick glance at Alex, who took the clue from her husband.

"Jahedah, I'm Alex, and this is my colleague Brady. We have a few questions for you before you're released."

Jahedah stared blankly at them for a moment and then looked down while she played with her head covering.

"Do you speak English?" Alex asked.

Jahedah didn't even move.

Hawk tapped Alex on her arm. "I'll take over now."

"Jahedah," he said in Arabic, "can you tell us what you're doing in Istanbul?"

She looked up and nodded before responding in her native tongue. "I'm here to visit a friend of my mother's. She told me of a marriage prospect."

"You are a widow?" Hawk asked.

She nodded.

"I'm sorry to hear that. What happened?"

She hesitated for a moment. "I—I don't like to talk about it."

"I understand. That can be a painful memory to discuss. Was it recent?"

Jahedah nodded again and glanced down at her hands, which were clasped and resting on the table.

"Do you have any children?" Hawk asked.

Tears welled up in Jahedah's eyes before streaking down her cheeks. Another subtle nod followed.

Alex reached across the table and placed her hand on top of Jahedah's and then offered her a handkerchief. Jahedah took it and dabbed her eyes.

"Thank you," she said in English.

Hawk wanted to be sensitive to the moment, but they needed answers. He hoped Alex's gesture would help warm their suspect to them.

"How do you know Evana Bahar?" Hawk asked.

Jahedah looked down, shielding her eyes with her right hand.

Hawk continued to press her. "It isn't a coincidence that you are from the same village as her in Afghanistan and that you passed for her on facial recognition, is it?"

She shook her head and looked up. After a deep breath, she composed herself and answered Hawk's question.

"Evana came to me in a time of need," she said. "After my husband Muhammad martyred himself, his death payment wasn't as much as promised. And one week later, my daughter was injured in a bombing at our market and lost her leg."

"I want to convey my deepest sympathies to you," Hawk said. "No one should ever have to endure so much pain, especially your daughter."

"Thank you," Jahedah said. "She's twelve years old now and needs another surgery that we can't afford. Evana told me that she would look after my family if I agreed to get a surgery so I would look like her. My daughter hated me for it, but it was the only way I could provide for her after Muhammad died."

"But you are still struggling?" Hawk asked.

"Very much so, even with Evana's help."

Hawk nodded. "Did she tell you why she wanted you to do this?"

"All she said was that if I got the surgery, I would have to travel from time to time for a few days. She said it would be like a holiday and that she would arrange for someone to look after my daughter while I was gone."

"Did she ever tell you that some people might mistake you for her?"

"She warned me this would happen, though it hasn't before. This is the first time, and it's terrifying."

Alex tapped Hawk on the shoulder and gestured for them to step outside for a moment.

"We'll be right back, Jahedah," Hawk said.

"What's going on?" Alex said. "I'm getting bits and pieces of this, but you know my Arabic isn't the best."

Hawk explained the situation to Alex. "What do you think we should do?"

"Let's turn her," Alex said. "She obviously needs financial help. We could use her to find Evana."

"That's a good idea. It sounds like Evana is using Jahedah as a human smokescreen to sneak into countries."

"And once someone thinks they have Evana, they stop looking for her. A genius idea, if you ask me. I can't believe no one else has ever thought of this."

"Let's not keep her waiting," Hawk said. "I'll make her an offer and see what she says."

They returned to the room and sat down across from Jahedah.

"You're a brave woman," Hawk said. "You're just trying to help your family, and I find that to be an admirable trait. However, I'd also like to help you if you would be willing to help us."

Jahedah cocked her head to one side. "What would I have to do?"

"We want to place a tracker in you so we'll be able to tell where you are at all times. So, if you're coming into a country, we'd know it and would prevent you from going through this type of interrogation again. You would be placed on a clearance list and could spend your time in peace wherever Evana sends you. How does that sound?"

"I might be willing to do that, but Evana is extremely suspicious. She has me scanned every time I meet with her. I'm not even allowed to see her until I've been approved by some of her men."

Hawk sighed. "Let me think about this for a minute." He explained the situation to Alex, who came up with another suggestion.

"What if you gave us a signal each time you entered customs?" Hawk asked.

"A signal?"

"Yes, a subtle gesture with your hands that wouldn't be natural so we could tell it was you. That way we could still track your entry into foreign countries but Evana would never know it. It'd be our little secret."

Jahedah rested her chin on her knuckles and studied Hawk and Alex. "And what exactly will you do for me?"

"For starters, we can give you a monthly stipend in an account overseas that Evana would never be able to learn about," Hawk said. "We also could get your daughter that surgery she needs with some of the best doctors in the world. How does that sound?"

A faint smile crept across Jahedah's lips. "That sounds most kind and generous, certainly not what I was expecting to hear from you."

They discussed what the signal would be. While checking in with a customs agent, Jahedah was to rub her left arm and form a circle with her thumb and index finger while doing so. It was just unnatural enough that anyone watching surveillance feeds would be able to identify her as the double.

Hawk and Alex then went over their contact protocol and how they would make plans very soon to pick up Jahedah's daughter and take her to the United States. Jahedah suggested her brother also go on the trip.

"We will need to verify all of this first," Hawk said. But once we do, we'll arrange for everything."

"Thank you," Jahedah said. "I'll look forward to hearing from you."

Turkish officials reunited Jahedah with her luggage and escorted her out of the office.

"Do you think that will work?" Alex asked.

Hawk shrugged. "Time will tell, but I think that was our best option given the circumstances. If that woman is telling the truth, she's been through more than any one person should have to endure in a lifetime."

"I just hope she's sincere."

* * *

JAHEDAH LUGGED HER suitcase behind her along the cobblestone streets as the sun dipped beyond the horizon. The streetlights flickered on as she hustled toward her hotel.

She felt relief over having survived the first encounter that Evana warned her would happen. However, Jahedah had a choice to make: Report the offer to Evana or keep it to herself. Jahedah thought she might be able to negotiate a new deal with Evana after informing her of the Americans' offer. Or

Jahedah could play both sides to get what she ultimately wanted—her independence.

As she pondered what to do, she heard footfalls echoing behind her. She quickened her pace before darting around a corner and breaking into a sprint. Yanking her bag off the ground, she clutched it against her chest and raced around another corner. She spotted a dumpster to hide behind and waited.

Moments later, two men dressed in suits came to a stop in the intersection of the alleyway. They craned their necks as if they were searching for someone. After a few seconds, they both dashed off in another direction without saying a word.

Jahedah's eyes widened.

What have I gotten myself into?

CHAPTER 5

Puyuhuapi, Chile

TITUS BLACK PALMED his gun as he crept out of bed. The alarm clock across the room displayed the time in glowing red letters. It was 4:37 a.m., far too early for any activity in the hotel hallway. Black had become acquainted with the resort's schedule for a time such as this. With the way his mind worked, he wouldn't be able to go to sleep until he understood the lay of the land—or in this case, the daily itinerary.

The flight out of Puyuhuapi occurred every morning at 8:30 and was a small prop plane. Passengers were only required to arrive a half-hour before takeoff. No other tours in the area started before 7:30, and breakfast wasn't served until 6:30.

The creaking along the floorboards outside Black's room persisted. He stuffed pillows beneath his cover and fluffed up his beanie to give the appearance of his head. Meanwhile, he settled into a prone position at the foot of the bed and waited for his room door to open.

A key slipped into the lock and turned, releasing the deadbolt. Clad in dark-blue uniforms, two men crept in, guns trained on where Black would've been asleep. Rolling over on his side, Black watched as the two men fired off several rounds at the bed. By the time they realized they'd been had, Black had fired a few shots. One man took two bullets, one to the chest and the other to the head. The other assassin dodged the headshot but had been hit in the chest.

Black rose from his position to make sure both men were dead. One of the men staggered backward before slumping against the wall. The other one who'd only be shot once grabbed his chest and growled as he made a run at Black. Caught off guard by what seemed like a sudden resurrection, Black spun to fire off another shot but was tackled and lost his grip on his gun.

The two men rolled around, getting in body blows and quick jabs while they knocked over chairs. Black found himself covered in blood as the injured assassin didn't seem bothered by his gunshot wound, fighting just as fiercely as anyone else Black had ever taken on in close-quarters combat.

In an attempt to end the scuffle, the assassin scrambled toward Black's weapon. Seeing the scene unfold, Black dove onto the man's back, pinning him to the ground. Black wrapped his arms around the man's head and twisted, snapping his neck and ending the threat.

Black panted as he stood and surveyed the carnage in his room. He needed to work quickly to dispose of the bodies before any early morning workers caught him. After pondering how to proceed, Black remembered he'd seen several fishing boats beached on the shore in front of the resort. He wrapped the bodies in bed sheets and shuttled the men downstairs on a luggage cart. Dragging the corpses into a boat, he found a few large rocks and rope. He weighted the bodies down and rowed out to the middle of the sound before sinking the two failed assassins.

Upon returning to his room, Black locked his door again and finished cleaning up the blood off the hardwood floors. When he was satisfied that it wasn't evident that two men had bled out there, he fell onto the bed and went back to sleep.

His phone rang, waking him up about an hour later. Fortner was on the other end.

"Hello," Black said.

"Titus Black, I hope I didn't wake you."

"Surprised to hear my voice, aren't you?"

Fortner chuckled. "Pleasantly so."

"You just tried to have me killed, and you're

laughing about it as if this was something you do in your leisure time. You sicken me."

"Actually, I was hoping you'd pass the test," Fortner said. "I really like you, Titus."

"What kind of sane person arranges a test like that?" Black asked. "I used to have a lot of respect for you as a general, but you've lost whatever sense of decency you ever had."

"If it's any consolation to you, I would've let your sister go if you didn't survive."

"Your time will come," Black said.

"Our time will all come one day. It's just a matter of when."

"For you, it will be sooner rather than later."

"As for you as well," Fortner said. "Now, regarding the matter of your sister: Will it be sooner or later for her? What will you choose?"

"What makes you ever think I'm going to help you?" Black sneered.

"For all your altruism, I have a difficult time believing you still don't see the world as it is, which is far more gray than black and white. Embrace the gray, Mr. Black."

"And what if I decided to help you?"

"For one thing, Laura would live," Fortner said. "And you'd have a very bright future within Obsidian. I'd make sure you were protected."

"From what?"

"There's a reckoning coming, and what you choose will have great consequences one way or another, consequences that will have an immediate effect on your sister's life. You must simply decide if are you in or out and deal with the fallout."

"Suppose I agree to help," Black began, "what will my first assignment be?"

"A simple one, really. I need you to tell me everything that Brady Hawk and the Phoenix Foundation team is doing. Where are they going? Who are they pursuing? What are their next targets? Think you can do that?"

"You want to eliminate Hawk, don't you?"

"We want him eliminated, yes, but at the time of our choosing. And you might be called upon to do just that. Can you handle that?"

"Of course."

"So can I count on you?"

"I'm in," Black said. "You how to reach me."

He hung up the phone and sighed. While he was relieved that Laura would be spared, he couldn't help but lament what saving her life meant he would have to do. Black never envisioned having to make such an excruciating decision when he entered this profession, but he never really hesitated.

He wasn't sure he would ever forgive himself for what he was about to do.

CHAPTER 6

Washington, D.C.

TWO DAYS LATER, the Phoenix Foundation team reassembled in the conference room to discuss next steps for how to proceed with Frank Stone. President Young wanted a ceremony in the White House's Rose Garden, touting how the U.S. would not be intimidated or bullied by anyone. With a grand display, Young wanted to show off Stone and talk about how the U.S. military was making great strides in beating back the bastions of terror. "Outing terrorists at every turn" was a phrase Young ran on, and he couldn't wait to show the fruit of employing such tactics. But not everyone was in favor of such a braggadocios claim, particularly since the terrorists always seemed to keep U.S. interests abroad on their heels.

Then there was the matter of how to handle the revelation that Evana Bahar was employing a body double to help her glide in and out of foreign countries with ease. It was a delicate situation for certain with Blunt unsure that the woman could be trusted.

Hawk settled into his seat next to Alex and sifted through an intelligence report on all of the latest Al Fatihin activity. There were rumblings of another strike in the U.S., though there was too much chatter according to Blunt.

"When we capture this much discussion about an attack, it's almost a sure sign something else is being planned," Blunt said as he gnawed on his cigar. "It's a classic distraction tactic that we need to be wary of. When Al Hasib struck our embassy in Kirkuk, all we heard about for weeks was a potential mission taking place in Afghanistan. At the time, we even transferred some of our agents to Kabul to see if we could get a more definitive location. But it was all just one giant smoke screen."

"That seems to be how Evana Bahar has chosen to get a leg up on our intelligence," Alex said. "She leaves breadcrumbs in one direction only to be lying in wait elsewhere."

"That's why I'm somewhat concerned about this body double," Blunt said. "How do we even know that you weren't actually talking to Evana Bahar? What if someone switched the DNA records in the computer? Or what if she paid someone to make such a bold claim?"

"I plucked a hair from the brush in her bag just to check myself," Alex said. "When I got back, I tested it and it didn't come back a match."

"What if that was planted?" Blunt asked.

Hawk sighed. "We could play this game all day, but when I looked into her eyes, I saw something I'd never seen in Evana's—I saw warmth. And you can't fake that."

"What about everything else?" Blunt asked. "Did her story check out?"

Alex nodded. "I tasked a CIA field operative in Afghanistan to look into the woman's claim about her daughter. And according to the report I received back, that was all true. Her husband was a suicide bomber and her daughter was injured in a market bombing and had her leg amputated. I'm not saying it would be impossible, but it's not likely she could've concocted a story like that and convinced so many people to go along with it. Our agent spoke with nearly a dozen people reportedly close to Jahedah, and they all verified her story."

"What about her brother?" Blunt asked.

"That's true as well," Alex said. "She has a brother, Ahmed, who lives next door and has been taking care of Jahedah and her daughter. According to her neighbors, Jahedah's situation isn't quite as dire as she made it out to be with Ahmed helping her, but it isn't rosy. And her daughter's health is a serious concern."

"So what do we do?" Black asked. "If we bring the girl to the U.S., that's inviting all kinds of problems."

"We're not inviting anything but an opportunity to demonstrate the goodwill that our country has, that we're not monsters," Alex said. "This is why we do what we do. We eliminate evil so that good may flourish."

Blunt nodded. "Alex is right. Evana Bahar is going to be searching for a backdoor into the U.S. if that intelligence chatter is accurate. But I'm not convinced that it is. Knowing her, she's got an entirely different agenda and she's forcing us to allocate our resources to one place so she can roam free in another."

"Then where?" Alex asked. "What else have we heard?"

"Maybe we need to go speak with Frank Stone again," Hawk said. "He might know something else other than just a meeting with Orlovsky in Istanbul."

"Hawk, go see if you can get anything else out of Stone," Blunt said. "Anything standard operating procedures might be nice to know too, especially before we venture behind enemy lines."

Hawk stood and nodded.

"So we're going to get the girl?" Alex asked.

Blunt nodded. "If Jahedah is doing what she says she's doing, we need to give her a show of faith. We need her to trust us and for her to know that we care about her before we ask her to do something incredibly difficult."

"Like what?" Alex asked.

Blunt shrugged. "I'm not sure at this point, but it could be anything from slipping Evana Bahar poison to telling us her next mission location. What happens next with her will determine where we go from here."

"And when do you want us to retrieve her?" Hawk asked.

"Within three days," Blunt said. "We must act quickly before she suspects that we aren't who we claim to be."

"I'll make it happen," Hawk said before he strode out of the room and went to pay Frank Stone a visit at a CIA black site just outside of Washington.

* * *

TITUS BLACK SHIFTED in his seat as he stared at the monitor on the wall behind Blunt's chair. A map appeared on the screen and zoomed in on Puyuhuapi, Chile.

"Now that the president's pet project has morphed into something more than just a simple extraction, we need to follow where this is leading us,"

Blunt said. "However, I don't think we can afford to ignore what Obsidian is doing. That organization is working so quickly that the trail might go cold if we stand idly by. And on that note, I want Black to fill us in on what happened in Chile with Fortner."

"Thanks," Black said as he stood and walked over to the monitor. "One day I hope to go back to Chile and relax while I'm there, but my hunt for Fortner turned out to be more stressful than I ever imagined."

"Did you find Fortner?" Alex asked.

Black shook his head. "But trouble found me in the way of a couple of mercenaries who were apparently hunting me. They told me that there was a bounty placed on my head. And while I couldn't get a name out of them, I figured them to be Obsidian goons."

"How close of a call was it?" Blunt asked.

"They broke into my room in the middle of the night and ambushed me. Fortunately, I heard the creaking down the hallway and was prepared when they entered. It was a harrowing experience."

"And you took care of your own cleanup?" Alex asked.

"I always do. They're both fish food now at the bottom of the channel."

"But you never heard from Fortner or saw him while you were there?" Blunt asked again.

Black shook his head.

"Damn it," Blunt said as he slammed his fist on the table. "I thought we had that little weasel this time."

"I think he had to know I was coming," Black said.

"What makes you come to that conclusion?" Alex asked.

"I know he had been there because I showed his picture to a bartender one night and he pointed me in the direction of where he said Fortner lived. When I arrived there, the place had been cleared out. Even the animals were gone."

"Surely in a small community like that someone saw something," Alex said.

"That's what you would think, but he lived in a secluded section of the mountain. You wouldn't know it was there if you didn't know where to look for it."

"Great," Blunt said sarcastically. "Now we're back to square one when it comes to Obsidian and Fortner. I'm sure the general's capture would be welcome news for the president even if it weren't something that could bolster his approval ratings."

"The real prize is uncovering the leadership of Obsidian without them knowing it so we can dissect the organization and eliminate them one by one," Black said. "And we're going to need to get far more creative if we're going to do that successfully."

Blunt inspected his cigar for a moment before jamming it back into his mouth. "And how creative are you talking?"

Black shrugged. "I'm thinking we employ one of Evana Bahar's signature moves here."

"Meaning what?" Blunt said.

"We figure out a way to make contact and mix a little fact in with fiction, maybe even volunteer to give up some people."

Alex scowled. "In exchange for what?"

"Whatever Obsidian can provide us that we would find valuable," Black said. "Maybe a place within their organization or some monetary compensation. I don't know."

"That's a dangerous game," Blunt said. "And I don't like putting our people at risk like that. We'd basically be sending our agents into a kill box every time and hoping for the best. That's no way to bring down an organization."

"Like I said, you tell them just enough to earn their trust and then—"

"I don't like it," Blunt said as he shook his head. "Evana Bahar might be willing to play that little game because she views all her people as expendable; they're just pawns on her chessboard. But I still hold fiercely to the perspective that all our agents are people,

people with loved ones and dreams. And I refuse to inject them into a situation where they don't have the upper hand. We all know the risks involved with what we do here, but I'll be damned if I'm going to tilt the board in favor of one of these terrorist punks."

Black nodded. "I understand, sir. I'm sure we'll figure out another way."

"Just find Fortner," Blunt said. "Now go."

"Before I do, can I speak with Frank Stone?" Black asked. "I have some very specific questions for him about Evana Bahar's operation procedures."

"Fine," Blunt said. "Go talk to him, and let me know if you learn anything useful. Then it's back to finding Fortner before the trail goes cold."

"Roger that," Black said. He exited the conference room and hustled downstairs. His phone buzzed as he got into his car.

"This is Black."

"Ah, my favorite soldier," Fortner said.

"What do you want?"

"I want some information. Since you're just now leaving the Phoenix Foundation offices, I figured now might be a good time to catch you and hear what you discussed. So, where is Brady Hawk off to next?"

"Nothing's been set in stone yet."

Fortner grunted. "I would strongly advise against lying to me."

Black sighed. "You're going to have to trust me."

"No, you're going to have to tell me the truth," Fortner said.

There was a pause followed by a woman screaming. Black only had to hear a few seconds of it before he knew it was Laura.

"I swear to you, I will hunt you down and—"

"The truth," Fortner said. "Where is Brady Hawk headed next?"

CHAPTER 7

Garmsir, Afghanistan

THE PLANE'S TIRES BARKED for a second before settling smoothly onto the unlikely runway located in the burgeoning city of Garmsir. During the height of the war in Afghanistan, the allied forces built a temporary base here along with a state-of-the-art runway. Once they left the region, the Afghanis recognized what a valuable asset a well-kept tarmac was when it came to attracting new business exploits. And even Hawk was surprised of the small airport. In all his travels across the Middle East, he couldn't remember a landing so smooth as this one, especially for an airfield that wasn't even on any non-military maps.

With Black assigned to resume his search for General Fortner, Hawk was accompanied by two CIA operatives, Langston Vaughn and Bull Truman. They were both respected within the agency and experienced with multiple missions in the Middle East. Even though Hawk viewed them as inferior to Black, they still helped ease the Phoenix Foundation operative's mind when it came to handling the assignment.

On paper, the job was a simple one: Escort Jahedah's daughter and brother back to Washington. But Hawk couldn't help but feel a sense of anxiety. Every time he set foot on Middle Eastern soil, he wound up fending off threats and attacks, often from out of nowhere. And despite Blunt assuring him the mission was a simple taxi ride in an airplane, Hawk wasn't so sure.

"Why do you look so pale?" Vaughn asked Hawk. "Are you nervous?"

"The last time I was here . . ." Hawk stopped himself. He wanted to connect with his two fellow operatives, but he also wanted to get the entire thing over with so he could get back home."

"What happened?" Vaughn pressed.

Hawk waved him off dismissively. "It was nothing. I'll be fine. I always seem to lose a little bit of my appetite after a long flight like that."

"Put something in your belly," Truman said as he threw an apple at Hawk. "We've still got fifteen minutes before we're scheduled to make contact with anyone."

Using his shirt, Hawk polished the piece of fruit before crunching into it. After a couple minutes, he'd devoured the whole thing.

"That was fast," Vaughn said. "You really should eat more while we're in the air next time. You might find flying more enjoyable."

Hawk flung the core into the trashcan across the cabin. "It's not the flight that makes me ill; it's the destination."

"Bad memories here?" Bull asked.

Hawk peered out of the window. "This is my first time in Garmsir."

"I meant Afghanistan," Bull explained.

"Let's just say if I never came back here again, it wouldn't bother me in the least bit."

"Fair enough," Bull said.

"So, do you know how this is going down?" Vaughn asked.

"Why don't you go over it one more time with me just so we're clear," Hawk suggested.

Vaughn nodded. "We're going to park by the small tower and get inspected. Once the airport authority clears us—meaning we fork over a large enough bribe—we'll be allowed to start adding passengers. Bull is going to handle that part. But you and I will march about a quarter of a mile north to the access terminal and retrieve Jahedah's daughter and brother. Then we'll promptly return to the plane, refuel, and get the hell outta Dodge. Simple enough?"

Hawk nodded. "Sounds simple, but I've been around these parts enough to know nothing ever goes as planned."

"Well, today is going to be the day that all changes," Vaughn said. "We'll barely be out of this plane more than five minutes."

The plane came to a stop by the traffic control tower just as Vaughn had explained. Toting a briefcase, Bull lumbered down the steps onto the tarmac, passing several parked vehicles before entering the office. After a couple of minutes, he reemerged with a knowing nod.

"Let's go," Vaughn said to Hawk.

After checking his weapon one final time, Hawk followed Vaughn outside. They strode across the runway, which was empty. As Hawk scanned the area, he didn't see another plane in sight, not even in front of any hangars.

"Who flies into this place?" Hawk asked.

"Not much of anyone now that the base has pulled out," Vaughn said. "But the people here are committed to making this an enticing feature for any businesses considering setting up shop in Garmsir."

Hawk surveyed the area once more, which eerily quiet, too quiet for his taste. "I've got a bad feeling about this."

"What do you mean?" Vaughn asked. "There's literally nobody here."

"That we can see," Hawk said. "Are you a parent, Vaughn?"

"Random subject change, but I've got a three-year-old son and a little girl on the way."

"You ever been in the house with your son and he's in another room and suddenly everything goes quiet?"

"That's happened numerous times."

"And what was going on?"

Vaughn chuckled. "Let's see. One time he was marking on the walls with crayons. Another time he was dumping all the shampoo out in the tub. And then once he was taking a dump in the hallway."

"They're at their worst when it's too quiet. I feel like I'm walking into a shootout in an old Western."

Vaughn waved dismissively. "I studied the satellite images for this airstrip for the past two weeks. It's a virtual ghost town. This is how it always was."

"Alex, can you hear me?" Hawk asked, activating his coms.

"Loud and clear," she said. "I'm watching you right now."

"And what are we looking like here? Anything to be worried about?"

"Not from what I can tell. There are a few heat

signatures near the lone terminal gate. But that's to be expected. That's where Jahedah's daughter, A'isha, and her uncle, Tamir, are supposed to meet you."

"Just keep me posted, okay?" Hawk said. "Something feels off to me."

Hawk and Vaughn arrived at the terminal and spoke with a man wearing a Garmsir airport badge. Vaughn reached inside his coat pocket and produced a document, which he handed to the man. After a few seconds, the man looked up and motioned over to a colleague, who opened a door on the far side of the room. Moments later, A'isha and Tamir appeared. With her arm around her uncle, A'isha limped forward. Hawk couldn't imagine how difficult life had become for the young girl in a country that wasn't anywhere close to accommodating for her condition.

"Thank you," she said as she reached the two American agents.

Hawk looked at the man standing by the terminal access door. "We need to get a cart for this girl," Hawk said in Arabic.

The man scowled. "This isn't the Kabul airport. We don't have a cart. She'll have to walk."

Hawk sighed. "You don't have anything we could use?"

The man shook his head and gestured toward the door.

"Is it okay if I carry you?" Hawk asked. "We have a long ways to go."

She shook her head. "I can make it."

Vaughn spoke briefly with Tamir, while Hawk held out his arm for A'isha to steady herself.

"You're a brave girl," Hawk said. "Going to a new country can be a frightening experience no matter how old you are, but especially if you do it as a kid without your parents."

A'isha didn't crack a smile, staring intently at the ground in front of her as she plodded along.

They continued on in silence and had reached the midway point when a loud noise behind them arrested Hawk's attention and made him spin around to see all the commotion was about. Driving wildly onto the tarmac was a truck loaded with masked men shouting and waving their rifles.

"We've got a big problem," Hawk said. "We need to run."

He scooped up A'isha and started running toward the plane, outpacing Vaughn and Tamir for the first few yards. Then gunshots pierced the air.

"Everybody get down," Hawk instructed.

He sank to his knees and helped A'isha lay prone as bullets sprayed all around them.

"Truman, can you hear me?" Hawk asked.

"Loud and clear," Bull said. "What's going on?"

"Look outside the damn plane," Hawk said. "We're under attack."

Bull hustled down the steps and onto the tarmac before taking only a second to survey the scene. He rushed over to a nearby Jeep and jumped behind the steering wheel. Moments later, he was roaring toward their position.

The terrorists were still far off but rapidly approaching. Hawk glanced at both vehicles and realized the terrorists were going to arrive first.

"Stay down," Hawk said to A'isha. He inched over toward Vaughn. "We need to provide Bull with some cover or else he's not going to make it."

Vaughn nodded as the two agents shifted their positions, looking south toward the oncoming truck.

"Go for the tires," Hawk said. "We need to slow them down."

Both men fired as more shots peppered the area from the swerving truckload of terrorists. Finally, one of Hawk's bullets found its mark, puncturing the front left tire. The loose rubber flapped on the runway as the vehicle continued driving toward them.

The flat had slowed the truck down enough that Hawk figured Bull was going to arrive first. It also gave Hawk a better chance to hit another tire. Steadying his weapon, he took aim again. His third shot found its target. This time instead of charging ahead, the truck slowed, teetered, and then careened onto its side. Men spilled out onto the tarmac, some of them getting knocked out by the blow. But not all of them.

By Hawk's count, five men weathered the crash in good enough condition to continue their assault. They sought cover behind their overturned vehicle as Hawk and Vaughn reloaded and continued to fight back. After a few seconds, an agonizing scream pierced Hawk's ears. Glancing behind him, he saw Tamir clutching his shoulder as blood spilled onto the ground.

"Stay down," Hawk said as he turned his attention back to the hostiles about a hundred meters away.

Bull whipped his Jeep in front of Hawk and Vaughn, leaving the vehicle running and using it to shield them from incoming fire. He dove to the ground to help A'isha and Tamir get inside.

"Come on," Hawk said. "We need to move."

Bull helped A'isha inside, settling her into the back as quickly as possible. Tamir stood upright, prompting shouts for him to get down by Vaughn and Hawk.

"Stay low," Hawk instructed.

Tamir didn't react fast enough, taking two bullets to the chest. He collapsed to the ground.

Hawk cursed under his breath as he looked into Tamir's wide eyes.

"I'm going to die," Tamir said.

"No, you're not," Hawk said. "Just focus on me. I'm going to get you out of here."

"Don't lie to me," Tamir said.

Bullets continued to skip all around them, some of them pounding the vehicle.

"We need to go," Bull said as he climbed behind the steering wheel. He leaned down, offering his hand to Hawk, but the hulking CIA agent rolled onto the tarmac when a shot ripped through his skull.

Tamir screamed again in panic. "We're all going to die."

"Stay calm, and keep your head down," Hawk said as he helped Tamir into the backseat.

Meanwhile, A'isha had crouched into the fetal position with her head buried in her hands. She was muttering a prayer between heaving sobs.

"I'll cover you while you get in," Hawk said to Vaughn.

Vaughn nodded and made a dash across the seats before using the passenger side door as a shield while he fired back at the terrorists. One of the men wrestled with his gun when it jammed, giving Vaughn a clear shot. He didn't miss, drilling the man in the chest and sending him toppling over the side.

Hawk didn't want to leave Bull behind, even if he was already dead.

"I know you're in the moment, Hawk," Alex said over the coms, "but I want you to know there is another truck loaded with terrorists heading your way right now."

"Thanks, Alex," Hawk said as he hoisted Bull's body into the back across Tamir and A'isha.

Hawk fired a couple more shots at the terrorists before ramming the Jeep into drive and peeling out of there. He kept his head down, just barely high enough to see over the dashboard. More bullets flew past, pinging off the vehicle as they accelerated toward the plane.

"Whatever you do, just stay down," Hawk said.

Tamir couldn't help himself. He turned around and raised up to see the scene behind him. That's when another shot struck him in the head. He fell over dead instantly, evoking more hysterical screams from A'isha.

Hawk and Vaughn rushed her into the plane before dragging Bull inside as well. With Tamir already dead, Hawk saw no reason to bring him along.

Even before the door was closed, the pilot spun the plane around and taxied down the runway. They didn't wait for any confirmation from traffic control as they raced to get airborne. Once the plane soared skyward, an RPG whizzed past the wing.

"What the hell was that?" Vaughn asked.

"That was Afghanistan," Hawk said.

Vaughn glanced down at Bull. "Damn it. He was such a good man. How am I gonna tell Judy about this?"

"The words never come easy," Hawk said.

"What happened out there?" Alex asked over the coms.

"We were ambushed," Hawk said.

"I don't know where those people came from," Alex said. "I didn't see anything close to that number of heat signatures until you left the terminal. They must've been masking it somehow."

"Well, whatever they did, it worked," Hawk said. "And, unfortunately, we lost a good agent and Jahedah's brother, Tamir."

"I can't believe this," Alex said. "Jahedah set us up."

"Maybe," Hawk said. "I just don't know why she'd do that if her daughter was with us."

"What other explanation is there for this?"

"I don't know right now," Hawk said. "All I know is that they knew we were coming."

CHAPTER 8

THE NEXT AFTERNOON, Titus Black visited the CIA safe house where Frank Stone had been holed up while acclimating himself to life as a free man. The initial psychiatric evaluation on Stone by the agency recommended that he take some more time before being thrust back into everyday life. Meanwhile, President Young was itching to marshal Stone into the Rose Garden for a photo op and a victorious press conference. And raising the tension even more was Stone's strong desire to get back to his normal life after being undercover for so long.

Black heard shouting as he approached the front door.

"I was held as a prisoner for six months by terrorists, and now I'm starting to feel like that all over again—in my own country," Stone yelled.

Black knocked on the door, knowing that his

intrusion would be a welcome relief to the agent receiving the brunt of Stone's ire.

The door swung open, and an agent greeted Black at gunpoint. "Let me see some identification."

Black held out the credentials Blunt had secured for the team while interacting with the CIA.

"Come on in," the man said. "We've been expecting you."

After a brief respite, Stone's tirade continued the moment the agent strode back into the living room.

"Just calm down, Frank," the agent said. "We have someone here who wants to speak to you."

"I don't want to talk to another shrink, damn it," Stone said. "I want to go home."

Stone grabbed a lamp off one of the end tables and ripped the shade off. He hurled the porcelain piece against the wall, shattering the bulb and the lamp.

Black held his hands out in a calming gesture. "It's all right, Frank. I'm not a shrink. I just want to talk."

"I'm done talking. I want to go home."

"Hold on a second," Black said. "I've got something for you."

Black hustled out to his car and dug a six-pack out of a cooler in the back of his trunk. When he returned, he was met with a scowl from the agent at the door.

"He's suffering from PTSD," the agent said in a hushed tone. "No alcohol allowed."

"Come on, man," Black said. "The man needs to loosen up a little bit. Let the guy have a beer. I'll leave one for you too."

The agent sighed. "Fine, but not in the house. I'm not being held responsible for this."

Black nodded before calling inside. "Meet me on the porch, Frank."

He settled into a rocking chair and removed two bottles. Digging out a bottle opener from his pocket, he cracked the tops off. The screen door creaked before bouncing shut as Stone wandered onto the porch.

"Well, it's not freedom, but a beer is pretty high up on my list of requests that I haven't been getting from these goons."

Black laughed and held out one of the drinks. "Have one and sit a spell."

Wrapping his hand around the beer, Stone eyed Black cautiously. "Why are you here? And what do you want?"

"I want the same thing as you—freedom. And if we don't put a stop to those thugs running around the Middle East foisting their radical ideals on a third of the world's population, we may soon be in the battle for our lives. Everybody loses then, chiefly our way of life."

Stone laughed before taking a swig of his drink. "I've been around those people quite a bit lately, and I wouldn't exactly say we're at DEFCON 5 yet. There isn't enough of them, and they aren't sophisticated enough to create any momentum. They can cause chaos and get everyone running scared, but they can't sustain a movement."

"Not yet anyway, which is exactly what we're trying to prevent."

Stone shrugged. "There are bigger fish to fry."

"Yet you gave up your life to infiltrate these people."

"Just because I don't see them as a threat to take over the world doesn't mean I don't think they need to be stopped. They're still out there killing innocent people—and to what end?"

Black scanned the woods surrounding the house. The sun streamed through the trees, while birds flitted back and forth from limb to limb and in the nearby brush. Cutting his eyes over at Stone, Black wondered how far he could push the former Al Fatihin prisoner.

"What was Evana Bahar like?" Black asked. "Did you ever have any dealings with her?"

"Yeah, she interrogated me several times. Once she hooked me up to some electrical system and shocked me every time I didn't give her the answer she was looking for."

"So how did you get her to stop?"

"I got better at lying."

Black drained his beer and then placed it on the table next to his chair. "Tell me again how you learned about Evana Bahar's trip to Istanbul."

Stone pursed his lips and looked out in the distance. "How many times do I have to tell everyone this? It's not that complicated to understand. I was locked in a room that had a vent in it, and the mine had an extensive ventilation system as you might imagine. I could hear everything they were saying during their meetings."

"And you didn't hear any other useful information other than her proposed trip to Istanbul?"

Stone nodded. "That's right. They didn't meet at this hideout very often."

"According to our satellite surveillance, she was holed up there for more than three straight months."

"Oh, she never stayed there that long. She was always coming and going."

Black furrowed his brow. "How could you know that since you were detained during that time?"

"I just knew, okay? I had infiltrated Al Fatihin long enough that I figured out how they operated under her command. She would never remain in one spot for very long."

"Then how can you refute what our intelligence officers found?"

Stone shrugged. "There's more than one way to sneak out of a facility."

"I don't know if I believe you," Black said. "All your wounds were superficial, unlike anything we've observed on previous Al Fatihin prisoners. And your intel seemed like some spoon-fed information just to distract us from what Evana Bahar is really up to."

Stone narrowed his eyes. "What are you trying to say?"

"I think you're carrying out an assignment for Evana."

"That's bullshit and you know it," Stone said. "If you knew anything about me, you'd know I would never betray my country."

Black dug into his back pocket and produced a folded up piece of paper. "Then explain this to me."

Stone snatched the document from Black. "What is this?"

"An offshore bank account in your name that received deposits while you were allegedly a captive."

"Where'd you get this?" Stone demanded. "This doesn't belong to me. Someone is feeding you lies."

Black stood, looming over Stone. "I beg to differ. The only one dealing in lies is you."

Stone leaped to his feet and shoved Black, who

stumbled back against the balcony. He set his feet and sprang into a defensive position. Escalating the confrontation, Stone delivered a flurry of punches, most of which Black fended off.

The noise from the fracas attracted the attention of the two CIA agents inside. They rushed out and grabbed Stone, subduing him and ending the altercation.

"Don't get too comfortable with your freedom," Black said.

Stone lunged at Black again but was restrained by the two guards. "I don't know who you think you are, but you're making a mistake coming after me. When I do get out of here, you'll find out what it's really like to be targeted."

Black nodded and glanced at the other two agents. "Did you hear that, gentlemen? Seems like Mr. Stone here has some more issues to work through before he's turned loose."

"Get inside," one of the agents said as he nudged Stone toward the side door.

Black grabbed the rest of his six-pack and headed toward his car. Once inside, he took a deep breath and turned the key, igniting the engine. Black didn't know how much longer he could go with his secret bottled up. Coping with the weight of what he was doing required that he talk to somebody about it, preferably someone who would understand.

He pulled out of the driveway and drove down the road for a few minutes before his cell rang with a call from Blunt.

"How's the search for Fortner coming along?" Blunt asked.

"It's coming along, but there's something I need to get off my chest," Black said.

"What is it?"

"I'm just now leaving the CIA safe house where Frank Stone is being held."

"And? Did you get anything new out of him?"

"Frank Stone is lying."

CHAPTER 9

Washington, D.C.

HAWK AND ALEX STOOD outside their car parked on the tarmac, awaiting the arrival of a special flight from Afghanistan, when Hawk's phone rang. Blunt's name materialized along with a picture Hawk had snapped of his boss with a cigar hanging out of his mouth. The image always made Hawk smile.

"Does he know you took that picture?" Alex asked.

"He posed for it," Hawk said. "It was the night after we caught Karif Fazil, and Blunt was a little excited."

"Excited for him is euphoric for the rest of us," Alex said. "I wonder how he celebrated the Astros finally winning the World Series."

"Probably a quick fist pump and a glass of scotch," Hawk said before answering the phone.

"Are you still waiting on Jahedah's flight to land?" Blunt asked.

"Yeah. She's supposed to be here in about twenty minutes. Why? What's up?"

Blunt cleared his throat. "I've got some good news for you."

"Lay it on me," Hawk said. "I could use some good news after that debacle in Garmsir."

"Interpol just arrested Evana Bahar."

"Seriously?" Hawk asked. "So soon? I thought Stone's intel was shaky at best, maybe even planted."

"Apparently not," Blunt said. "She didn't give the signal at the customs agent. They even ran her prints through the database."

"Why would she be so brazen?" Hawk asked.

"It was a brilliant scheme," Blunt said. "Apparently she wanted to change the way she traveled from country to country, which we believed in the past was through various private jets at smaller airports, which allowed her more flexibility to get in and out of places. But by using a body double, facial recognition systems will remove a person from the searchable images until the person exits the country. That allowed her to go in after Jahedah without getting flagged."

"Something about this still seems fishy."

Blunt sighed. "Hawk, stop trying to ruin my moment. I called you to commend you on a job well done."

"You pump your fist and drink a glass of scotch?"

"What?"

"Never mind," Hawk said. "Forget I asked that."

"I still want you to be vigilant with Jahedah, just in case there's something else at play here."

"What? Like a third woman who was surgically altered to look like Evana?"

"You really are trying to spoil this victory, aren't you?"

"It's Al Fatihin," Hawk said. "There's never a moment where you can rest on your laurels and enjoy a win. They are always trying to make our lives chaotic and do a pretty good job of it. If we don't stay alert, we're going to see a lot of innocent people suffer. And I'm not about to let that happen."

"Good," Blunt said. "Just follow protocol. It shouldn't be an issue, but I wanted to give you a heads up."

"So, what are they going to do with Evana Bahar now?"

"There's a long list of countries trying to extradite her for crimes against them. Turkey is one of the few places that hasn't charged her with anything."

"We probably won't even get a piece of her," Hawk said with a sigh.

"England trumps us when it comes to the statutes filed against her. We have to take our place behind them. Honestly, I'm not sure she'll ever have to come here and answer for what she did."

"I can't believe she outsmarted herself," Hawk said. "But she was bound to get caught one day. I only wish I'd been the one to do it."

"Well, you helped make it happen," Blunt said. "Now, you and Alex do something better than catching a terrorist—help an innocent girl who's been maimed by a terrorist."

"Thanks for the heads up. I'll call you later once everything is taken care of."

Hawk hung up and turned to Alex. "We did it."

"We?" she said, casting him a playful sideways glance.

"Well, Blunt said we made it happen after turning Jahedah last week. It's not as fun as bringing her in myself, but it's still a thrill to know that we were part of the operation that eventually led to her demise."

"But Al Fatihin is still out there—and very active from all the chatter we've been hearing lately."

"It'll take a while for them to recover from this," Hawk said. "At the very least it gives us a reprieve, not to mention a chance to do the kind of good that I haven't done in a very long time."

Alex's phone buzzed with a text message, and she read the note on the screen before pocketing her cell.

"What is it?" Hawk asked.

"Jahedah's plane is making its final approach. She'll be on the ground any minute now."

"Is your equipment ready for the DNA test?" Hawk asked.

Alex nodded. "We'll be able to tell if we got a match within a half hour. It'll take that long for us to process her here anyway, so she won't notice any delay."

Fifteen minutes later, the jet rolled up to the hangar and powered down. Once the engines had wound down for a few seconds, the door opened and the steps unfolded, Jahedah made her way to the ground and kept her head down as she strode toward Hawk and Alex.

Alex greeted Jahedah with a smile and ushered her into an office. Hawk stayed so he could translate.

"I'm sorry about your brother," Hawk said in Arabic. "Tamir seemed like a good man. We did what we could to save him, but someone knew we were coming and ambushed us."

Jahedah took a deep breath. "I'm confident you tried to help him. It's just most unfortunate. But I am grateful you protected my daughter. It would've been a cruel fate to die on her way to America in a battle after getting injured by a bomb. It's like she's cursed."

"We managed to break the curse," Hawk said. "Now, Alex here is going to need to do a DNA test.

There's nothing to be afraid of, but we want to verify you are who you say you are. I'm sure you can understand our paranoia."

"Of course," Jahedah said. "I'm not offended by such a request."

"Would you mind rolling up your sleeve then so Alex can withdraw enough blood to run a test?" Hawk asked.

Jahedah cast a wary glance at him.

"It won't hurt," Alex said.

Hawk translated what she said and nodded at her. "You'll just feel a tiny little pinch, but you'll be fine."

Alex smiled while extracting the blood, and Jahedah responded in kind. When Alex finished, she capped the two vials and left the room for her testing kit, which was set up in an adjacent office.

"She'll be right back," Hawk said. "In the meantime, we've got plenty of paperwork to process."

Hawk was joined by a pair of State Department officials who worked through all the documents necessary to get Jahedah a visa to be in the U.S. for a couple weeks.

"Can we hurry this along, guys?" Hawk asked. "Jahedah's daughter is scheduled to undergo surgery later this afternoon."

"We'll do this as quickly as possible," one of the men said as he looked over the top of his glasses at Hawk.

Satisfied that Jahedah was in safe hands, Hawk went to visit Alex. She said the check wouldn't take that long, but it had been more than twenty minutes and he hadn't heard from her.

"What's going on?" Hawk asked.

"This stupid computer is running slow. Honestly, I don't know why I always forget that the machines out here are from the ice age."

"Well, I think they're close to being done," Hawk said.

"Okay, okay. I can't make this thing go any faster."

No sooner had she snipped at Hawk than the computer beeped, signaling the completion of the results. Alex clicked on the machine and scrolled down the page.

"Well, what is it?" Hawk asked.

"That's not Evana Bahar," Alex said slowly as she cocked her head to one side.

"And it is Jahedah, right?" Hawk asked.

"Yes," Alex said. "It matches the sample we took from her in Istanbul."

"Then why do you look like you aren't necessarily convinced?"

"Nothing really. It's just that there's something odd about one of these markers."

"But you're positive that's Jahedah?"

"Yes," Alex said. "Everything matches what we had before. I even compared it to Evana's DNA just to be sure. And that's definitely notEvana Bahar."

"So, all's good."

"It appears that way. Sorry, it's just been a long day, and I'm a little rusty on my parsing of DNA data."

"Great," Hawk said. "I'll go pass along the news to the two agents who are going to be watching her while she's here."

Several minutes later, Jahedah completed her paperwork and Hawk released her into the custody of a pair of agents.

"I want to see my daughter first," she said.

"We can arrange that," the agent in charge said before escorting her out of the room.

Hawk followed them. "Alex and I will stop by for a visit tomorrow, Jahedah."

She smiled and waved before getting into the back of the car with the two operatives.

* * *

LATER THAT EVENING, Hawk was sitting on the balcony of his apartment with Alex, the two deciding which latest Bollywood film they were going to watch.

"So, what's it going to be?" Alex called from the living room. "Happy Phirr Bhag Jayegi or Mulk? A comedy about two sisters or a thriller on terrorism?"

"I think I've had my share of terrorism for this week. Why don't we watch the rom-com?"

Alex chuckled. "Look at you going all soft on me."

"I just need to laugh, something I haven't done much of lately."

Alex handed Hawk a beer before clinking bottles with him. "Then let's hope Happy Phirr Bhag Jayegi lives up to the hype as one of the best Bollywood comedies of the year."

Hawk arranged for the movie to be streamed to their television. Seconds later, the movie opened with a scene that had both of them laughing hysterically. But it was all put on hold when Hawk's phone buzzed. It was Blunt.

"Let me pause this," Hawk said.

Alex shot him a glance.

"It's Blunt," he said. "You know we have to take this."

She sighed. "Fine. Just make it quick. Remember, we need to laugh."

After less than a minute of conversation, Hawk hung up the phone. All the color had vanished from his face.

"What is it?" Alex asked.

"The CIA called Blunt to let him know that when the shift change came at the safe house, the other two agents were found dead in the living room and Jahedah was gone."

Alex shook her head. "That wasn't Jahedah who flew in here today. That was Evana Bahar."

CHAPTER 10

THE NEXT MORNING, PRESIDENT YOUNG greeted Mike Mitchum, his brand new chief of staff, who was one of Capitol Hill's rising young stars. With the president's ratings lagging among younger voters, Young wanted a fresh face, someone who had a commanding presence but could also bring innovative ideas to the table. In all of the focus groups Young's staff conducted, the biggest complaint among the next generation of voters was how old everyone looked and how they never seemed to deviate from the status quo.

But Mitchum was transforming that perception. The former Army Ranger had served in the Middle East yet had a knack for creating viral videos that could make a point with humor. His foray into Washington politics as a freshman representative was heralded as a game-changer. And it didn't take long for Young to snap him up with an offer for the coveted position.

Young wanted to get his daily security briefing as well as discuss the plans for the rest of the day and that evening's State of the Union address.

"So, how are we going to wow America, Mike?" Young asked.

Mitchum shrugged. "Be amazing as always, sir. We're still in the middle of transitioning from being a reactive administration to a proactive one, not to mention we're still dealing with the fallout from the National Security Complex dedication."

"I thought that was all behind us. That was months ago, which might as well be years in Washington."

"To us, perhaps," Mitchum said, "but to the average voter, that's still the latest scandal. However, there's something else we have to worry about now."

Young's eyes widened. "What is it now?"

"Evana Bahar, the leader of Al Fatihin. She's here."

"In the country?"

"In Washington," Mitchum said.

"How the hell did we allow that to happen?" Young asked with a growl.

"I'm working to get more details for you, but apparently she tricked some of our agents here into thinking she was someone else. The details don't matter as much as the fact that there's a real threat tonight."

Young smirked. "There's no way she could ever touch me tonight. The Capitol Building during the State of the Union address is probably the safest place to be in America, especially when they see who the designated survivor is."

"Sir, as a result of this news, I'm not so sure we shouldn't cancel the speech."

"What on earth for?"

"We're going to have most of our security forces focused on protecting you. It'd make us vulnerable in so many other places."

Young waved dismissively. "She'd be a fool to come to the Capitol Building tonight."

"Still, I think it's something you should seriously consider."

Young stood to pace around the room. "Mike, I hired you to give me creative ideas, not to try and dissuade me from delivering an incredible speech that will unite the country."

Mitchum broke into a soft laugh.

"What's so funny?" Young asked. "Do you see this all as some big joke?"

"No, sir. It's just that State of the Union addresses have zero chance of bringing the country together. That's pie-in-the-sky thinking right there. We need to use this platform to fire up our base and give the world a chance to see what kind of man you really are. You can take control of the narrative here, not the critics."

Young nodded confidently. "That's right, which is why we're not about to postpone the address."

"Okay, fine," Mitchum said. "In that case, let's fight terrorism by showing how this country is the antithesis of terrorism."

"Absolutely. What stunning idea did you have in mind?"

"Well, there's this girl from Afghanistan one of my staffers suggested we put on stage with you tonight," Mitchum said. "She lost her leg in a market bombing by a terrorist. But two of our agents brought her here to allow her to have a surgery she desperately needs to prevent her from losing the rest of her leg and to fit her with a state-of-the-art prosthetic."

"Sounds like a damn fine idea," Young said.

"Only problem is she's from the same village as Evana Bahar."

"Why's that a problem?"

"I don't know. Just going with a hunch this could be some sort of elaborate scheme by Al Fatihin."

"For the last time, I pay you for good ideas and winning over the next generation, not your hunches. Besides, I trust that our incredibly competent law enforcement personnel will catch Evana Bahar before the speech—and we'll find a way to work that into the final iteration, won't we?"

"Of course, sir," Mitchum said.

"Now when that happens, do you think we should slide that bit of news in at the beginning or use it as part of the speech's crescendo? I'm not sure I could wait for half an hour to report that we just captured the same woman who tried to kill me a few months ago."

"I'll figure out a way to make is splashy," Mitchum said. "That's my job, remember?"

"Get FBI Director Creston Taylor on the phone," Young said into the intercom on his desk. "I need to find out where his agents are with apprehending Miss Evana Bahar."

"Right away, sir," his secretary replied.

A few seconds later, she reported that Taylor was waiting on the line.

"Cres, how the hell are you?" Young asked. "I've been meaning to give you a call."

"Just another day in paradise defending our cyberspace and snuffing our old school criminals," Taylor said.

"Well, I wanted to get an update straight from the horse's mouth about the search for Evana Bahar. Have you started closing in on her yet?"

"Not yet, sir, but we've diverted a substantial number of resources in the area toward finding her.

We're coordinating this manhunt with the CIA."

"That's good to know," Young said. "And I trust you'll be able to apprehend her very soon."

"That's the goal, sir. We want to arrest her before anyone else gets killed or even hurt."

"If there are any more developments, will you let me know straight away?"

"Of course, sir. I'll pass along updates as soon as they're available."

"Excellent. I'm counting on you, Cres."

Young hung up and asked for Mitchum to leave for a moment. Once he was out of the room, Young used his private and secure cell phone to call J.D. Blunt.

"What the hell is going on with Evana Bahar?" Young asked.

"News travels fast," Blunt said.

"Do I need to be worried?"

"We're working on it right now. She used some kid as a decoy to get in. I'm not sure how much of the story I believe anymore."

"Are you talking about the girl from Afghanistan who needed surgery on her amputated leg?" Young asked.

"That was in the briefing too?"

"Actually, I just heard about it from Mitchum. We're thinking about inviting that girl on stage at some point during the speech to show that America can be both a fierce defender of freedom around the world as well as a compassionate nation. Is there anything wrong with a move like that?"

"The girl is twelve years old," Blunt said. "I'm not sure what she could do to you. But there's always the danger you run of inciting violence from the radicalized Muslims who will never forgive you for using the girl to promote some sort of compassionate democracy. If I were you, I'd find another way to communicate that same message."

"I'll think about it," Young said. "Though you have to admit, it'd be a killer move when it comes to changing the hearts and minds of those around the world who perceive us as some evil nation."

"Look, Noah, I'm not a political strategist, and I'm not going to try and dissuade you from doing something that could be considered as benign as that. But if Evana's plan here includes using the girl in some way, maybe as a propaganda tool, the short term political gain might not be worth it."

"Well, it's your job to make sure nothing comes of it," Young said. "I want the girl on the stage—and I want Evana Bahar's head on a platter as the cherry on top."

"You can't always have it all," Blunt said. "But we'll do the best we can."

"That's all I can ask," Young said before he hung up.

But that was a lie. Young wanted to ask for more. Ultimately, all he really wanted was to become popular again, something he never imagined he'd ever pursue after winning the presidency. But here he was, doing whatever it took to become popular just so he could remain in office like his predecessor.

Blunt's wrong. I can have it all. And I better get it tomorrow.

CHAPTER 11

TITUS BLACK WAS ON HIS way to the NSA to meet with an analyst to go over some communiqués they found of General Fortner when Blunt called. Black stared at the screen for a moment, unsure that he wanted to answer it. He wanted to figure out who was holding his sister and where so he could go exact justice on the traitorous Fortner.

What now?

"What are you doing today?" Blunt asked.

"I'm going to the NSA which flagged some recent activity related to Fortner. I want to see if I can pick up the trail again on him."

"That'll have to wait. There's been a change of plans."

"Come on," Black said. "You know the longer we let this go, the more our chances diminish of finding Fortner again."

"You know I wouldn't do this unless I absolutely need you to."

Black sighed. "Of course. What happens to be so pressing now?"

"It's Evana Bahar. She's in Washington."

"How the hell did she get into the country?"

"The short answer is she and her body double pulled one over on us."

"Then what about the girl? Isn't she here now too?"

"Yes," Blunt said. "And the president wants to put her on stage with him during tomorrow night's State of the Union address."

"Is he out of his mind?"

"He's desperate, trying to cobble together every scrap of political capital he can find."

"And he thinks having some girl from Afghanistan that we've helped will do that for him?"

"I think this is all Mitchum's doing," Blunt said. "That guy thinks more about social media views than he does about the effect the policy is having on the country. And make no mistake about it, the president will get a nice bump in his favorability ratings after showcasing America's goodwill in front of the entire world. But it also opens him up to some other sort of danger."

"Evana Bahar is using that girl somehow."

"That's what I think," Blunt said. "I just don't know how yet."

"And that's what you want me to figure out?" Black asked.

"Actually, I want you to start surveillance on Capitol Hill. Scout out any locations in the chamber where Evana Bahar could've already been or how she might hide."

"Isn't security already tightened up the week before the speech?"

"This woman is capable of sneaking past even the most stringent protocols, so I'm not sure some extra security is going to keep her out. She somehow changed her DNA files in the Homeland Security database, so I won't feel comfortable until that speech is over, especially with that girl standing next to Young."

Black got off at the next exit and headed back toward downtown. "I understand. I'll see what I can do."

"I want you to scope out the place as if you were going to assassinate the president. I mean, it's not like you haven't done this before."

"That was a long time ago," Black said.

"But I'm sure what you learned then will give you a good starting place now."

"Okay, I'm on it. I'll give you a full assessment later today."

"Excellent," Blunt said. "I know we'd rather not

be wasting our time protecting the president from his own stupidity, but hopefully it won't cost us a shot at finding Fortner."

"Roger that."

Black mulled over how he would assassinate the president during a high-profile speech on national television—and get away with it. If it was a suicide mission, the chances of succeeding were much higher. But Black knew Evana Bahar was narcissistic enough that she wanted to revel in her victory and use the moment to propel Al Fatihin's agenda. However, he wasn't sure that was her reason for being in Washington. There were plenty of other targets for her to go after that would provide ample benefit to her cause.

No, Evana Bahar wants immortal fame. She's going after Young.

Black displayed his credentials to the parking attendant at the Capitol Hill deck before parking. He removed his weapon from his trunk and checked all the pieces. If he could sneak his rifle inside while entering as a normal citizen, he would have serious concerns about the level of security.

He hustled up the steps and strode into the line for the metal detector. Removing his jacket and belt, he placed them on the conveyor belt along with his briefcase. The first two objects breezed through the scanning process, but the guard inspecting the x-rays paused for a long time on the bag housing Black's rifle. After a few seconds, two of the agents conferred with each other before starting the belt again.

"Sir, is this your case?" one of the security personnel asked.

Black nodded.

"I need you to come with me for further inspection."

"Sure," Black said.

Maybe this screening process is tighter than I thought.

The guard dropped the briefcase onto the sterile metal table and opened the lock. He poked around inside for a few seconds before taking a small piece of cloth and wiping down random areas inside. Once he finished, he placed the swath into a machine and waited. Ten seconds later, a beep signaled the end of the analysis.

"You're all clean," the guard said as he handed the case over to Black. "Now you're good to go. Have a nice day."

Black smiled and nodded. "Thank you."

Unbelievable.

He grabbed the handle and resumed his ascent up the steps. Meandering around the upper floor of the chamber, Black maneuvered past a couple guards.

He already knew the blind spots in the security system, which hadn't been changed in years.

Black worked his way along the catwalk, avoiding detection from the man patrolling the upper floor.

If I was going to do this, I'm not sure I'd change a thing from several years ago. This is still the best blind in the chamber.

Black eased into a prone position and pretended as if he was going to sight in the president at the podium.

Then his phone buzzed.

I swear I'm never going to get a moment of peace.

The number was blocked. Black got to his feet and shuffled across the catwalk to a nearby storage room. Once inside, he answered the call.

"This is Black."

"Titus, it's so good to hear your voice," Fortner said.

"Listen here, I won't be at your beck and call twenty-four hours a day," Black said. "If you've got something to say, save it until—"

"I just texted you a link. Open it."

Black glared at his phone and swiped to his message. After tapping the link, he watched a live webcam feed appear on his screen. His sister was struggling to get away from a man wielding a knife. Her hands and feet were bound, and her muffled screams could still be heard despite having a gag shoved into her mouth.

"I think you need a gentle reminder that you'll do as I say," Fortner said.

The man with the knife went up to the camera, looking into it with wild eyes and made a throat-slashing sign with his knife while grinning.

"I don't know what you think you're doing, Fortner, but you're going to pay dearly for all of this, that much I can guarantee you," Black said.

"More empty threats and idle promises," Fortner said. "Your sister's life literally depends upon you doing what I say, and you continue to behave as if you somehow have control over what's happening. Here's a cold dose of reality for you since you're not exactly getting this through that thick skull of yours: I am in charge, and you will do as I say or your sister will die. Are we clear?"

"What do you want?" Black asked.

"Nothing really. I just need you to assassinate the vice president."

"Sure thing," Black said. "I'll squeeze that in after my morning run."

"Tomorrow night during the State of the Union speech, I want you to shoot the VP."

Black sighed. "That's a suicide mission."

"Is it now?" Fortner said. "I believe you've gotten away with murdering someone in the chamber before."

"This isn't the same," Black said. "If I do this, I

won't."

"If you don't, your sister dies. It's a simple choice."

"And a strange one. Why not have me kill the president instead?"

"It's not your place to question the assignment. You just need to complete it."

Black chuckled. "That's because you aren't really calling the shots, are you? You're just passing along orders from someone higher up the food chain. And once you've worn out your usefulness, you'll become expendable, just like you think I am."

"I find your speculation amusing. If you want to share all your conjectures with me instead of fulfilling the assignment, I'll just kill you and your sister and move on."

"Fine, I'll do it," Black said. "But after this, I'm done."

"You'll be done when I say you're done," Fortner said with a growl. "Just be ready for my signal."

Black hung up and exhaled, seething over the impossible situation he'd found himself in. And no matter how hard he tried, he couldn't shake that image of Laura from his mind, the sheer terror she was experiencing, the trauma Fortner had wrought upon her with one of his goons.

Black needed to find a way to flip the tables on Fortner—and fast.

CHAPTER 12

HAWK AND ALEX ENTERED the Phoenix Foundation offices and marched upstairs to the conference room. Blunt was already waiting for them along with CIA Deputy Director Randy Wood. While Blunt snipped the end off a cigar and then jammed it into his mouth, Wood stirred his cup of coffee.

"What's taken you two so long?" Wood asked. "This meeting was supposed to start five minutes ago. Did you two fight over which route to take to work?"

Alex rolled her eyes and then looked at Blunt. "You're actually friends with this guy?"

"Cordial acquaintances," Blunt said. "I'm not quite ready to start sharing my scotch with him, especially the expensive kind Hawk brings me. Well, the kind he used to bring me."

"Sorry. I didn't get a chance to shop at the duty-free store and pick some up for you on my last trip to Afghanistan," Hawk said. "I was a little busy trying not to get murdered."

"You obviously succeeded," Wood said. "Now, let's get on with this meeting before Evana Bahar lights the city on fire."

Hawk and Alex sat down across from Wood, who was seated on one corner next to Blunt at the head of the table.

"Proceed," Hawk said.

"Now, I reached out to J.D. because you two know the inner workings of this terrorist cell as much as anybody, Frank Stone withstanding," Wood said. "Even though we can't risk tying the two of you to the CIA's official search for Evana Bahar—especially with the FBI involved in this now—you really need to be the lead agents on this case. At the risk of duplicating our efforts, I want you to feel free to conduct your manhunt and simply keep me informed about what you're doing. Or if you have other suggestions on places we should be looking for her, I'll send agents over to do that tedious work. But we have to cooperate on this if we're going to catch her before Young's speech tomorrow night."

"Unfortunately, the president is insisting on moving forward with putting A'isha on stage during his address," Blunt said. "I'm not sure we'll be able to dissuade him from that, so the next best thing is to capture Evana so we can breathe easy."

"Actually, thatwould be the best thing," Hawk

said. "The quicker we remove her from Al Fatihin's leadership, the better. She's more skilled than Karif Fazil when it comes to organizing a serious threat."

"How so?" Wood asked.

"Fazil was great at leveraging what he could into attracting more followers, but he didn't have the ability to pull off a massive culture-shifting attack like 9/11, even though he aspired to. Evana Bahar is smart and has friends all over the world. And on top of that, I think she's getting some help."

"From who?" Wood asked.

"We're not positive yet, but it appears that she's formed some strategic alliances with other groups to help further her cause," Alex said.

"Is this all speculation, or do you have proof?"

"At this point, we're still investigating these connections," Alex said. "But there seems to be strong evidence that points to her utilizing some of her relationships built while running her nonprofit in London."

"So, you're suggesting all those refugees weren't necessarily entering the country with peaceful intentions," Wood said.

Alex nodded. "I'm sure that isn't news to you, but until we started to grow suspect of her, she was a media darling. We just had no idea that beneath the surface, she was assembling the pieces for a global terrorism organization."

"How do we proceed?" Blunt asked. "I know you're a busy man, Randy, and we don't want to take up any more of your time."

"I'll forward you any leads we get the moment we get them," Wood said. "If you want to investigate any of them, I'll let you choose. If not, I'll let our people look into it. Do you know where you want to begin?"

Hawk nodded. "We'd like to visit Georgetown Hospital and speak with A'isha to see if Evana visited her. I know it might seem unlikely that she would go there given that the entire city is looking for her, but she's brazen and prone to do the things you wouldn't expect her to do."

"That's what makes her so dangerous," Alex added. "Her unpredictability is about the only thing you can predict when it comes to pinning her down."

"You should've taken your shot when you had the chance," Wood said.

Hawk widened his eyes. "What are you talking about?"

"You know exactly what I'm talking about," Wood said. "You tried to leverage her for some other fishing expedition you were going on, never realizing you had the shark in the boat before you released her back into the water."

"I suggest you stop right there," Blunt said as he glared at Wood. "Some of those issues are above your pay grade."

Wood sighed. "Fine. But if you get her in your sights again, just don't miss this time, okay?"

He gathered the stack of documents in front of him and then tossed them into his briefcase.

"We'll be in touch with a report as soon as we speak with A'isha," Hawk said.

Wood pushed his chair back and stood. "I look forward to working with you two."

"Good seeing you, Randy," Blunt said.

Wood sneered and left the room without another word.

"What did you do to him?" Alex asked.

"He still thinks I cheated the last time we played poker," Blunt said, waving dismissively. "That's just Randy. With a mind like a steel trap, the man knows how to hold a grudge. But I'll let him win next time and all will be forgiven. Now, you two better get going. We don't have any time to waste."

* * *

HAWK AND ALEX ENTERED the hospital and went straight up to A'isha's room where she was recovering from the surgery. A pair of agents stood outside her door and weren't about to let Hawk and Alex inside without authorization.

"Fine," Hawk said. "Call Randy. I just left a meeting with him."

"Sorry, sir," one of the agents said. "I have to check. I have a list, and your name isn't on it."

Hawk dialed Wood's number and handed the cell to the agent. After a brief conversation, the man handed the phone back to Hawk and apologized.

Hawk patted the man on the shoulder. "You're just doing your job. And I promise you that you need to be vigilant."

The man nodded and slid aside so Hawk and Alex could enter. Inside, they found A'isha sitting up in her bed.

"How do you feel?" Hawk asked in Arabic.

"Good," she said with a big smile. "I'm supposed to get my new leg this afternoon, and tomorrow I'm supposed to be on stage with the president."

"Welcome to America," Hawk said with a smile. "All your dreams can come true."

"Do you know when my mother is coming? I thought she was supposed to be here last night."

"Actually, she had a change of plans, but she's trying to get to you as soon as possible. Once she lands here, we'll make sure she gets right over here to see you."

"Thank you," A'isha said. "You've both been so kind. I can't tell you how grateful I am."

Hawk's phone buzzed. He glanced at the screen before locking eyes with A'isha.

"We just wanted to stop by and check on you," Hawk said. "Good luck with your new leg."

He turned to Alex. "We need to go."

Once Hawk was in the hallway, he answered the phone.

"Where are you?" Wood asked.

"We're at Georgetown with A'isha. But we're about to leave. What's happening?"

"There's a report of a woman who looks like Evana wearing a suicide vest who's roaming Pennsylvania Avenue. Do you want to check it out, or do you want me to send in some of my agents?"

"We'll take it," Hawk said. "Text us her last known location and any images you have of her."

"I'll have it all to you in a couple minutes," Wood said before ending the call.

Twenty minutes later, Hawk and Alex parked near the White House and raced to Pennsylvania Avenue. Law enforcement cleared the sidewalk along the street and kept tourists and other visitors from getting close to the famed presidential mansion. Wandering all alone was a woman who faintly resembled Evana Bahar.

"Do you think that's her?" Alex asked. "You've seen her up close more than I have."

"That woman certainly favors her, but I can't tell from here. I'm going to need to get a closer look."

"Did you bring your binoculars?" Alex asked.

"No, I need to get much closer."

"Seriously? Look at her. She's clearly crazy. That can't be her. Not to mention that she's obviously wearing a vest covered with explosives."

"You can see that from here?"

"Can't you?"

"I'm not going off any eyewitness reports until I've confirmed it for myself. I know how people are in this day and age. They see a bulge in a person's pants pocket and think it's a handgun. When really it's just a set of car keys."

"That's the twenty-first century for you. Everyone is paranoid. You can thank those 9/11 terrorists for that."

"You stay here," he said. "I'm moving in for a closer look."

Hawk moved stealthily toward the woman until he was about fifty meters away from her. The hood draped over her head shrouded her face.

"Evana, what are you doing here?" Hawk called as he crept toward her.

The woman looked up briefly and then put her head back down. She spun around and started to walk the other way.

Hawk pursued the woman as she weaved back and forth along the sidewalk. After a couple minutes, she stopped and Hawk darted closer.

"Evana!" Hawk called.

The woman turned around, and Hawk could see by the wrinkles around the woman's eyes that she clearly wasn't the terrorist mastermind.

"She told me you'd call me that," the woman said as she removed her hood. "She said—"

A bullet ripped through her shoulder before she crumpled to the ground in a heap. Hawk glanced at the woman to determine the direction from where the shot was fired. Given how quickly situations had escalated in the past between Hawk and Evana, he wasn't about to stick around and see if the woman was merely a distraction. He darted toward a row of trees and took cover behind one of them.

Five minutes passed before he fished his phone out of his pocket and called Alex.

"That's not Evana," he said. "And that vest isn't packed with explosives, not that it matters to that woman any more. She's bleeding out."

Alex cursed under her breath, just loud enough for Hawk to hear it.

"My sentiments exactly," he said. "Let law enforcement know she's not really a threat. I need to call Wood."

He hung up and stared at the woman, pitying her.

"Don't look at me like that," she said. "You can't imagine how I feel. It's what I had to do to eat today."

He found an image of Evana on his phone and held it up for the woman. "Was this the lady who approached you?"

The woman squinted, trying to see the image, and then nodded. "She paid me fifty bucks to walk around with this thing. It's made out of cardboard."

"Are you sure?" Hawk asked.

"It's just a bunch of cardboard boxes. See for yourself," she said as she ripped open her coat.

Hawk immediately noticed a countdown mechanism with a screen.

"No!" he yelled as he dove behind a tree.

Before he hit the ground, the vest incinerated the woman. Hawk couldn't even look. The scene was too gruesome.

His phone rang with a call from Alex.

"Are you all right?" she asked. "You're not moving."

"I'm alive," Hawk said. "But Evana Bahar has to be stopped right now."

CHAPTER 13

PRESIDENT YOUNG PACED around one of the rooms just off the House floor as he prepared to be introduced for the State of the Union address. Over twenty-four hours had gone by since he learned that Evana Bahar was in Washington. And while he had hoped to include her capture in his speech, she was still on the lam.

Mike Mitchum shifted through several pages of Young's speech before handing it to him.

"Is this going to accomplish what I want it to?" Young asked.

"I guess that depends," Mitchum said. "We couldn't include anything about the capture of Evana Bahar, but I think your average American will be impressed with the sympathetic tone you strike during this speech. You're going to tell the public that we want freedom and opportunities for everyone all over the world. And sometimes that comes at a great price. Then you conclude by telling them that in the midst of great suffering, hope blossoms. That's when A'isha walks onto the stage and you tell her story. It's going to be a viral moment that captures the attention of the nation."

"Let's hope so," Young said. "I'm tired of letting the media control the narrative about this administration and what we're about. We want to see Americans succeed. We want to see this country flourish. And unfortunately, we're just sustaining brutal attacks from lies conjured up by anonymous sources and White House insiders. I'm sick of it all."

"Well, I can promise you that this speech will definitely fire up your base and present a gentler side of you that will appeal to Independents," Mitchum said. "And if we're really lucky, that will be the dominant talking point for the next twenty-four-hour news cycle."

"I've never been that lucky in my life," Young said.

"I'm not guaranteeing that will happen, but it's possible."

"Well, I hired you to help reach the next generation of voters, not perform magic tricks."

Mitchum smiled. "The two aren't mutually exclusive."

Young paced around the room as he studied the speech. After fifteen minutes, he looked up at his chief of staff.

"So when am I finally going to get to meet his A'isha girl?" Young asked.

"Would you like for me to bring her in now?"

"Of course," Young said. "I'd like to make a connection before we parade her on stage like some kind of trophy."

"In that case, I'll be right back," Mitchum said before he exited the room.

Young's private phone rang with a call from Randy Wood.

"Is this a bad time?" Wood asked. "I thought I'd try to catch you before it got too close to the speech."

"Is there ever a good time to speak with me?" Young asked. "Honestly, it depends on what you want to say."

Wood sighed. "Look, I just want to make sure you aren't putting that girl from Afghanistan on the stage."

"Are you raising some new concern now?" Young asked.

"No, it's just that—"

"Stop being a Debbie Downer, Randy. Apparently, I have more confidence in your people than you do. Nothing is going to happen to me tonight."

"It's not likely, but I wouldn't rule it out. I'm just trying to err on the side of caution. Evana Bahar is a dangerous—"

"If I don't ever hear her name again, I'd be a happy man. Just make sure your people are extra vigilant tonight and let me inspire a nation with this speech."

"Yes, sir," Wood said. "I'll do my best."

Young hung up and flung his phone onto the couch. He interlocked his fingers and rested them on top of his head while circling the couch in the de facto green room.

How did I ever get into this mess?

A knock on the door interrupted his thought process, and then Mitchum slipped inside. He pushed the door open wide and looked behind him as if waiting for something. After a few seconds, A'isha shuffled forward with her state-of-the-art prosthetic leg.

"You must be the young woman everybody is talking about," Young said.

A'isha broke into a big smile when Young's gaze met hers.

"Sir, she doesn't speak much English," Mitchum said. "But I can bring in a translator for you, if you wish."

"Absolutely," Young said. "I want her to fully understand how grateful I am that she would be wiling to come on stage with me and show the harbingers of fear what it looks like when America reaches out and promotes the goodwill that has marked this country for more than two centuries now."

Mitchum darted out the door, returning after a couple minutes with a translator.

"Here you go, sir," Mitchum said. "This woman can convey whatever thoughts you'd like to pass along to A'isha."

Young spoke with the girl for a few minutes, letting her know how important her appearance on the stage was tonight and that the world would know all about her in the morning. She smiled, seeming to understand. When Young finished, she looked at the translator and said something.

"A'isha wants to know when she'll be able to see her mother?" the translator said.

Young furrowed his brow. "I'm not sure about that," he said. "Tell her as soon as she gets here. And ask her if she's uneasy about anything."

After a back-and-forth between A'isha and the translator, the woman looked at the president and sighed. "She said she's comfortable with going on stage with you. I told her that everyone would clap and that she'd have to stand and wave. Apparently, she's excited about the standing part of it."

"Ask her what happened," Young said. "To her leg, I mean."

A'isha dropped her head after hearing the

question. She held up her hand, a gesture to make the translator stop talking.

"Is everything all right?" Young asked.

"This is a delicate subject for her. She said there's been a lot of pain over the years regarding how she lost her leg. According to her, her father had a suicide vest attached to him in a public market where a lot of Allied soldiers were. Right before it exploded, he saw her and tried to stop the bomb, but she says someone else was controlling it and made sure he died anyway."

"Tragic," Young said. "This poor girl has been through a lot. I hope tonight is an opportunity for her to put to rest some of this pain for good."

"Me too," the translator said.

Mitchum knocked on the door as he pushed it open. "Sorry to ruin this for everyone, but if A'isha is going on stage tonight, her physical therapist needs to inspect her prosthetic leg once more."

Young smiled and gestured toward the door. "Go," he said. "We want to make sure you're well enough to spend a few moments in the spotlight."

A'isha didn't move, instead staring blankly at the president. The translator stepped in and explained everything, resulting in A'isha spinning toward the door and leaving the room without another word."

As the time for the speech drew near, Young popped a breath mint into his mouth, inhaling the fresh taste. Mitchum held open the door and ushered Young toward the stage.

"Are you ready, sir?" Mitchum asked.

"We've got to get it over with one way or another," Young said. "Let's just hope you and your genius ideas pay big dividends."

"There's only one way to find out, sir. Go knock 'em dead."

Young took a deep breath before striding toward the door that led to the main stage.

"And now, the President of the United States," an announcer boomed on the house floor.

Here we go.

CHAPTER 14

HAWK COULDN'T QUITE REMEMBER where along his journey as an operative that he added contortionist to his résumé. With as many times as he'd hidden in the trunk of a car, he considered that was the source of this skill that had blossomed into fine art. He sat on his haunches in a space about the size of acceptable carry-on luggage, though he was certain if he had been a suitcase, the flight attendant would've had to have put him away wheels first before slamming the door on his head. But Hawk still would've fit. The only thing extending beyond that space was the tip of his gun.

"Couldn't I have just stood against the back wall in the upper level of the chamber like everyone else?" Hawk asked over his coms. "No, Blunt thinks that if, Heaven forbid, anyone found out about us working in conjunction with the CIA that all the democracy in the universe would be at stake."

"How could you say such a thing?" Alex asked.

"If you had to be crammed into a small space like this, you'd be saying the same thing."

"No," Alex said. "How could you mistake the amazing design of our government for a democracy? Everyone knows our country is a democratic republic. There's a big difference between the two. It's like confusing a rifle with an RPG."

Hawk groaned. "Maybe I just say crazy things when as a grown man I'm being asked to fit into a spot that would be challenging for most toddlers."

"Consider it a character building experience for you," Alex said.

"There has to be a better way to build my character, much less protect the president," Hawk said. "Wouldn't my services be better served in some other capacity, like, I don't know, conducting surveillance like a normal human being? My legs don't collapse, and I certainly wouldn't be able to accept any glory for my marksmanship. I'd be surprised if I could hit a watermelon from point-blank range while all snug like this."

"It'll all be over with soon enough," Alex said. "Based on the transcript we received earlier, you're only going to have to stay in that space for the next hour and a half, maybe a little bit more accounting for applause and any rabbit trails Young leads us down."

"Alex, I'm shoehorned into a space about the size

of a box. I don't think I can stay in here another five minutes, much less ninety."

"You know it was necessary for the mission," Alex said. "We needed to keep you there in case another shooter took up a position in that virtual bird's nest. Trust me, the presence of security guards on Capitol Hill is triple what it usually is, so they've got plenty of people everywhere. This entire building is undoubtedly secure."

"I'd be careful of making such a sweeping statement, especially one of that nature," Hawk said. "If we were all certain that no one was up here, I wouldn't be here."

"You're there as part of an insurance plan," Alex said. "We're trying to make sure we've covered all our bases."

"Insurance plan?" Hawk asked as he shifted in the box. "Surely you could've come up with a better lame excuse than that."

"Look, it got you in the building, and we might need you. When the time calls for it, you can just shed the box and make sure you catch Evana Bahar."

"There's no way she's going to show her ugly face here."

Alex moaned. "What did you just say about making sweeping statements?"

"I've followed that woman for far longer than I

ever wanted to, and she's not about to risk everything she's built just to make a statement."

"Why not?" Alex asked. "It'd be a stroke of genius and a way to shake things up a bit recruiting wise for Al Fatihin. You're the one always saying that the only thing about her that's predictable is her unpredictability."

"Yes, but I don't think I agree with your presumption on what she's willing to do for the cause. She's above dying for it, at least when it comes to martyrdom. If there's anything she wants, it's to ascend to the throne as the leader of this movement. And she can't get there if she's dead."

"Regardless, keep an eye out for her up there, will you?" Alex said.

Hawk sighed. "Of course. I've got nothing else to do."

Below him, both Republicans and Democrats alike stood and applauded as President Young plodded up the steps. Hawk glanced at the scene and shrugged.

It's gonna be one big, fat I-told-you-so session when this is over—and I'm going to send my chiropractor bill to Blunt for the next three months.

A half hour into the speech, Hawk was still well secured, out of the sight lines of every person in the building. And he was bored as ever.

"This reminds me of a stakeout," Hawk said.

"Except it's without all the great food and coffee and bonding moments, which are the three best elements of a stakeout."

"Just keep watching," Alex said. "You never know when something might—"

"Alex?" Hawk called. "Alex, are you there? Can you hear me?"

"I'm here," she said. "Something just went funky with my monitor, well, all the monitors really."

"What is it?"

"I don't know, but the screen was acting really glitchy for a few seconds. But everything seems to be working fine now."

"Strange," Hawk said. "But maybe that also means you're the one who needs to keep an eye out for anomalies in the cyber world."

"There it is again," Alex said. "Hawk, my screen isn't working any longer. And neither are the other surveillance cameras."

"Don't worry, Alex," Hawk said. "That's why I'm here, remember? I'm your insurance plan."

CHAPTER 15

TITUS BLACK CROUCHED low, confident that no one could see him as he prepared to take aim on the target. On more than one occasion, Black was fairly certain that he was going to die, that no amount of marksmanship was going to get him out of a jam where he was outnumbered. He quickly learned that being a good assassin also meant trusting yourself and being creative in pressure-packed moments. Yet, he had never been more nervous about embarking on a mission of this magnitude.

The directive from General Fortner had been clear: eliminate Vice President Charles Bullock. However, Black wasn't inclined to turn on the very people he was supposed to be serving, even if they didn't know of his existence. To coerce him to do something so heinous required proper motivation—and Fortner had managed to collect droves of it. Wading into the weeds with a master spy was always ill-advised, something akin to playing checkers with a chess champion. As a result, Black's options seemed to be reduced to a single one.

Going along with Fortner would mean casting aside every ounce of integrity Black had left. His word would be rendered meaningless. His trust would be irrevocably broken. His future would be dictated by Obsidian's ability to take over the world—and he'd have to hope that someone there remembered what he did for them. But there were so many moving parts that Black even considered it a long shot. Fortner essentially had his hands around Black's throat, a quick squeeze away from eliminating him and searching for a new and more compliant assassin.

I always have a choice.

Black ascribed to that belief, but he wasn't sure if it was true. His reality was that his sister's life hung in the balance. Was he willing to lose his last living relative? The answer was a resounding no. He and Laura had been through so much together as kids, and letting her die wasn't truly an option. He had to do whatever was necessary to keep her alive. Once he did that, he could deal with Fortner.

Black pulled out his binoculars and zeroed in on the target. With no other variables to take into account, Black figured he could make a clean shot the first time. There would be no gory images to shake, no epic gunfight. One shot was all he needed.

Using his phone, Black watched the live stream of President Young's State of the Union address. Fortner warned that there would be a specific phrase to listen for late in the speech and once those words were uttered, that would be the signal for Black to take aim.

Listening with just the left earbud, Black heard Young's grandiose claims about what he'd been able to achieve in office over the past year. The list he rattled off was impressive, certainly one that wouldn't have warranted the approval rating of less than fifty percent. Young wasn't the most charismatic leader, but he had managed to convince Congress to compromise on several issues to get important legislation approved and turned into much-needed laws. While hearing Young deliver his impassioned speech, Black wondered how the president had strayed so far from his political roots of working for the benefit of the people. From all the inside information Black had, he could tell Young was now only working to maintain the fleeting power he still possessed.

Fortner called Black, interrupting the live stream feed.

"Are you ready?" Fortner asked.

"I'm in position," Black said. "Just waiting for the signal."

"Excellent. However, there's been a slight change of plans."

"What do you want now?"

"The same thing, except I will tell you when to take action."

"How's Laura?" Black asked.

"She's fine and anxiously awaiting for you to fulfill your side of the bargain. Once you complete the assignment, I'll text the address where you can pick her up."

Black hung up in disgust and resumed listening to Young's speech. While the president blathered on about how much progress the country was making under his leadership, Black couldn't help but let his mind drift. He felt helpless, stuck like a hamster in a wheel. Despite working hard to defeat power-hungry despots and wild-eyed terrorists all intent on dominating people to fatten their bank accounts or further their agendas, Black wondered if it would ever end. Was he simply weeding the world's garden, plucking one sadistic leader at a time only to watch another spring up in its place? He knew the world would fall into chaos if people like him didn't fight. But it was exhausting, especially when collateral damage became personal.

Laura just wanted to live a normal life as a librarian for the Library of Congress. She wanted to hang out with friends, encourage the next generation through education, and one day have a family of her own. But that dream was in serious danger. And for that, Black wanted to make sure Fortner paid a dear price, preferably with his life. In the meantime, Black was willing to play along.

Black peered through his scope and studied the target. Anger welled up in him, even in a moment when he knew he needed to be calm. This was never something he imagined happening. It's why he had passed on getting married, fearing that he would someday be forced into a similar situation. He never imagined Laura would get trapped in this twisted game.

Glancing at his phone, Black waited for Fortner's signal.

In one ear, Black listened to Young continue his speech, touting how the American dream had returned thanks to his robust economic policies. He talked about how the booming marketplace was better for everyone, not only in the United States but also abroad. Each one liner was mostly met with partisan praise or disdain as the cameras rotated between wildly cheering fans or petulant politicians, unwilling to admit that someone on the other side of the aisle actually had a good idea. In a few rare moments, his words elicited bipartisan applause. However, those were few and far between.

Black eased his finger onto the trigger. He was ready to pull it.

CHAPTER 16

PRESIDENT YOUNG ADJUSTED his tie while he reviewed his speech one more time. Mike Mitchum pulled Young's jacket taut and straightened the American flag lapel pin. In the corner, the White House photographer snapped a few shots of the last-minute preparations.

"Are you ready for this?" Mitchum asked.

Young forced a smile. "I'm always ready." It was a lie. His palms were beading up with sweat. After a deep breath, he winced.

"Is everything all right?" Mitchum asked.

"I started thinking about this speech and bringing out the girl from Afghanistan," Young said. "Do you think this is a good idea? As far as I know, Evana Bahar is still on the loose since none of our agencies have been able to apprehend her."

"It's always been risky, but not because there's terrorist lurking in the city," Mitchum said. "Some people might view it as a political stunt even though this type of compassion is consistent with your administration."

"What if we changed it?" Young asked.

"Well, you're the president, and you can make that call if you want to. However, the media already has a copy of this speech, and if you decide not to bring out A'isha, that alone might overshadow anything you have to say."

"We certainly don't want to have the message lost because of that. Tonight is too important of a moment."

Mitchum stepped back and inspected Young again. "Look, if you're uncomfortable with it, scratch it. You need to look as confident as you feel. Every twitch, every hand gesture, every word—they will all be parsed by the press corps and discussed at length in the coming days. If you falter here, it could spell trouble for the support you need to push your administration's agenda through this term."

"This is a tough decision, one I don't think I can win with either way. But I think I'll be much more at ease if she's not up there with me."

A knock on the door interrupted their conversation. Mitchum shuffled across the room to open the door. Another staffer spoke in a hushed tone with him.

"What is it?" Young asked.

"Sir, A'isha wants to speak with you before your speech," Mitchum said.

"I thought I told you . . ." Young trailed off as he saw the young girl appear in the doorway.

"Sir, here's A'isha," Mitchum said, ushering her in along with a translator. "A'isha, the President of the United States."

"Nice to see you, Mr. President," she said with a faint smile through the translator. "Thank you for all that you've done for me."

She strode toward Young, showing off her new prosthetic leg. After walking for a few feet, a wide grin spread across her face.

"I can even jump now," she said. "Would you like to see?"

Young couldn't help but chuckle, nodding as he did. "Of course, by all means show us what you can do now."

A'isha squatted and then leaped up, throwing her hands in the air and giggling. She stuck her landing.

"Impressive," Young said. "Is there anything you intend to do with your new leg now?"

"I want to play football," she said. "Not the American kind—real football."

Young nodded. "I understand."

"After the accident, I spent a lot of time watching my brothers while my mother was away at work. And all they did was kick the ball, but I could never play with them. Now, thanks to your country's kindness, I will be able to do that now."

"Your smile is infectious," Young said. "And I'm sure your story will inspire millions of people around the world tonight. War is a horrible thing, but the life that springs from darkness is stronger than we ever imagined."

"You sound like a wise man," A'isha said. "Your country is lucky to have you leading it."

She nodded respectfully, a gesture Young returned, before she spun toward the door and walked out.

Mitchum looked at Young. "Quite an impressive young lady, isn't she?"

"Forget it. I'm keeping her in the speech. And can I get a translator? I may even let her talk."

"Well, I wouldn't go that far," Mitchum said. "You don't want her to steal the spotlight from you, which a twelve-year-old girl from Afghanistan will undoubtedly do."

"Why not? She's polished, eloquent, and—"

"And she just flattered you. Don't let that distract you from the overall purpose of the evening, which I can promise you will be derailed if you let her speak into the microphone."

"Okay, okay," Young said. "She's just electric.

You know what I mean?"

"I do, but let's forget about that for right now and get focused on what you have to say to the American people."

* * *

A HALF-HOUR LATER, Young marched onto the stage amidst a tepid response, enthusiastic among his fellow party members, obligatory on the other side of the aisle. It looked like the beginning of every other State of the Union address for the past forty years, with the rare exception of a couple when Ronald Reagan held office.

After a brief welcome and introduction, Young launched into the heart of his speech. He implored Congress to enact legislation that would help the middle class while laying out an agenda for how he planned to strengthen Homeland Security and prevent terrorists from worming their way onto U.S. soil. Then he ventured into the most critical portion of his talk, tackling the five hundred pound gorilla on his back.

"What happened at the dedication of the National Security Complex recently has shaken every American I know, especially the accusation that I'm negotiating with terrorists. And I feel like I do owe the American people an explanation."

He paused to take a sip of water before continuing.

"There have been several occasions—I could count them all on one hand—where we felt like it was in our best interest to deal with terrorists in a non-traditional way. As a general rule, our nation has rejected attempted talks with radical extremist groups, no matter what leverage they claimed to hold over us. We will never be held hostage by demands. However, there have been a few select times when it was in the best interest of our country to broker a deal. That in no way should suggest that we've gone soft on terrorism or that we lack the constitution to do what needs to be done to defeat this abhorrent evil in the world.

"What does that mean to you, the patriotic citizen who cares about this country and the standard bearer of freedom that we've become on this planet? It simply means that we will do what's necessary to create an environment of safety for all Americans, both here and around the world."

Young's statement was met with lukewarm applause from both sides of the chamber. He studied the lawmakers and judges seated in front of him. Many of them shifted in their seats and wore furrowed brows. Others gazed around the room, trying to see how others were reacting to the news that America did indeed negotiate with terrorists whenever it deemed necessary. And while the news wasn't shocking since Young's tactics had already been exposed, many in Congress appeared concerned with the admission.

As Young read the room, he decided to curtail the next paragraph in his written speech, speeding ahead to the part where he introduced A'isha.

* * *

"HOW ARE THINGS LOOKING from your vantage point?" Alex asked Hawk over the coms.

"Nice and cozy here with no sign of activity whatsoever," Hawk said. "It's like a ghost town."

"I guess that's a good thing, right?"

"To be honest, I'd prefer to leave here tonight without firing a shot. And I'd consider that a good day at work."

"That's the gold standard."

"What about you?" Hawk asked.

Alex sighed, loud enough that Hawk could hear it.

"Is everything all right, Alex?"

"Well," she said, "it's just that I've been noticing some anomalies over the past half-hour in the security feeds, and I'm not sure what's going on."

"What kind of anomalies?"

"It's like a cyber attack of some sort, but it doesn't look like they're trying to insert a virus of any kind," she said. "To be honest, it looks like amateur hour. There's no real discernible pattern here, which usually suggests it's a wannabe hacker who's still learning the ropes."

"Takes a lot of guts to try and hack into the security network on Capitol Hill during the State of the Union address."

"Or stupidity, though they've done a good job at masking their location. I can't seem to find where these attacks are originating from."

"Is anyone else aware of this issue?" Hawk asked.

"I let the cyber security team know, but they're more focused on data mining attacks and protecting all these officials' privacy. Apparently, capturing dirt on opponents is a venture that pays big dividends."

"You say that as if you're surprised."

Alex chuckled. "I'm not. But it is the upside down world we live in. We're all about protecting our individual interests rather than banding together to protect the interests of others."

"If this spy thing doesn't work out for you, maybe there's a future for you in philosophy."

"There's no future for anyone in philosophy, at least if you want to be gainfully employed."

Hawk glanced around the room, checking all the visible entryways.

"There's still no movement here," Hawk said. "Meanwhile, Young is still rambling on."

"This is his moment. Just relax."

"Did you figure out what all those glitches were about?"

"I wish," Alex said. "In fact, they just started to intensify."

"What's going on?"

"Whoever was initiating these attacks has somehow gained control of the closed circuit feed."

Hawk glanced at the screen, which was still projecting a live image of Young at the lectern. "Well, there's nothing unusual on now. It's just Young talking. Can you stop what they're doing?"

"I'm working on it. Stay tuned."

* * *

PRESIDENT YOUNG TURNED to his left and held out his hand before gesturing for A'isha to join him on stage.

"One of the things I wanted to highlight tonight is our country's incredibly generous spirit," Young said. "This young girl from Afghanistan suffered horrifically when a Muslim extremist set off a suicide bomb in a marketplace in her hometown, killing more than a dozen people and injuring scores of others. Unfortunately, A'isha lost her leg in this attack."

As Young moved away from the lectern, she strode up the steps and took her place next to him out in the open so everyone could see her prosthetic leg.

"When some of our people in Afghanistan

learned about A'isha's story, they reached out to see if they could bring her here for a surgery. She couldn't afford one here or anywhere else in the world, but we offered the whole procedure for free. And now, I'm happy to show you what this has meant to this vibrant young girl. She will undoubtedly overcome the pain and suffering she's endured at the hands of violent lunatics, determined to force the rest of the world to bend a knee to their narrow-minded ideology. Her spirit is infectious, and I wanted to share her story with you tonight."

"Thank you, Mr. President," she said.

Many people on the chamber floor leaped to their feet. Even the most partisan members of the crowd couldn't help but stand and clap for the girl and what her story meant.

After a few seconds, Young held up his hands in a gesture to quiet the cheering. "America is not a bully. In fact, we're one of the few countries courageous enough to confront global bullies. We don't want to exploit our neighbors. No, we want to help them experience the incredible freedom and prosperity that has marked this nation since its inception."

Young didn't see the screen behind him flash. His image flickered in and out until it went dark.

"Ultimately, America is about—"

"To experience the consequences of its sins,"

boomed a loud, distorted voice over the sound system, drowning out Young. "Your president is a liar, and today he will pay for his crimes against the world."

Young stopped talking once he heard the voice and noticed everyone in the audience staring at the large screens flanking him. He turned toward the screen before looking back at the audience, which stared in disbelief.

Gunfire echoed in the hallway just outside the chamber doors, and chaos ensued.

* * *

BLACK'S EYES WIDENED as he stared at the unfolding scene. The image on the screen was of a person wearing a Guy Fawkes mask, speaking in a distorted voice.

"There's nothing wrong with your screen," the person said, the voice overpowering Young's amplified speech. "Everything is as it should be. Your president is a liar, and it is time that he pays for his sins against humanity."

The camera panned back and showed Young angrily shaking his finger at the screen and yelling something. But his microphone had been cut off, and his words were indiscernible. Moments later, the feed switched from the cameras in the chamber to the image on the projected screens behind the stage.

"Noah Young has gotten away with murdering

innocent people in the name of his so-called freedom for far too long with no accountability. Tonight, there will be a reckoning that will be unavoidable no matter how many children's prosthetic limbs he distributes. It's the least he could do since the young girl he ushered on stage was actually dismembered by a drone missile."

The feed suddenly switched back to the cameras, which were zooming all around the room as several armed gunmen stormed in. Black watched as guards suffered point-blank shots to the chest and head. But before the attackers could reach Young, members of the Secret Service rushed up and snatched him.

"Take your hands off Noah Young, or you will all die," the man said. "The little girl's prosthetic leg has enough explosives to level Capitol Hill."

The agents froze as the Al Fatihin operatives swarmed around Young.

"Lay down your weapons," the man commanded.

The men placed their guns on the ground with the exception of one who ignored the warning. He drew his gun up to shoot but collapsed as a sniper from the back of the room obliterated the man with a head shot.

"Any other wannabe heroes?"

Evana Bahar raced into the room and stood at the lectern. She fired off several rounds before a camera zoomed in on her.

"Let this day go down in history as the day that the U.S. president's transgressions were atoned for by his own blood," she said. She pumped several more bullets skyward before letting out a primal scream and gesturing for her men to follower her with Young in tow.

Black's phone buzzed. "You're up," Fortner said. "Take the shot."

Black steadied his rifle and stared through the scope at his target.

One, two . . . three.

Black squeezed the trigger, and a shot ripped through the glass window. Using infrared glasses, Black could see the man crumple. The other guard inside scrambled across the room, clearly surprised by the presence of an intruder. He stumbled right into Black's line of sight. Another shot, another guard fell to the floor.

Black scanned the area once more and raced toward the door, kicking it down.

"I said now," Fortner screamed.

Black hung up and raced into the makeshift prison site. He fired off a couple shots at the deadbolt, splintering the door. It swung open with a swift kick, and he wove through the dark hallways until he found Laura bound up in a room with only a cot and a bucket for her to relieve herself. She was delirious and pleading for him not to touch or hurt her.

"Laura, it's me, Titus," he said.

Her sobbing tapered off. "What are you doing here?"

"I came for you, Laura. It's time to go."

"But how did you—"

"I'll explain everything later," he said, helping her to her feet.

With her brow furrowed, she eyed him closely. "But you're not a . . . What are you?"

"Like I said, I'll explain everything later. But we need to get out of here right now."

Black's phone buzzed again with a call from Fortner. "What the hell are you waiting on? Pull the trigger now."

"I already did," Black said. He hung up and snapped a couple photos of the dead men lying on the floor. Attaching the images to a text message, he replied to Fortner:

I'm coming for you next.

Seconds later, Fortner replied:

You better not miss.

Black helped Laura into his car and sped away from the site. As he was driving, another call came in, this one from Blunt.

"Where are you?" Blunt asked. "I thought I told you to stay around Capitol Hill."

"You know where I am, don't you?" Black asked.

"Actually, I do—and you've got a lot to answer for. But that can wait. I need you to help Hawk. Evana Bahar and her Al Fatihin goons took Young."

"I know," Black said. "I saw the whole thing."

"Get over there with him as soon as possible and put in your coms. Alex is helping coordinate our side of things with the FBI and CIA, who are all about to lose their minds over this thing, wondering how it all happened."

"Evana Bahar played us all," Black said.

"I know. And we have to figure out what her next move is before it's too late."

"I think it's obvious what she's going to do now. We just have to figure out where she intends to do it."

CHAPTER 17

HAWK RACED TOWARD his car, weaving in and out of the members of Congress and other distinguished guests fleeing toward hopeful safety. The security team pleaded with everyone to stay calm, but their effort was largely ignored. With people screaming and yelling as they sprinted out of the building, law enforcement couldn't assess the situation properly. Meanwhile, media members swarmed outside with microphones and cameras, ready to capture interviewees willing to describe what it was like inside.

"Talk to me, Alex," Hawk said over his coms. "Where did these bastards go?"

"I'm trying to track them," she said. "Putting together a composite of the area right now and attempting to identify the vehicle they left in."

"Hurry it up. I'm almost to my car."

He pumped his arms and ran as fast as he could. His lungs burned as he gasped for each breath in the frigid Washington night air. Snowflakes flitted toward the ground, creating a slick veneer on the sidewalks and streets.

"The last thing we need right now is a snowstorm," Hawk said.

"It doesn't matter whether you need it or not because we're getting it," Alex said.

Hawk could hear her fingers flying across the keyboard as she muttered under her breath.

"What is it?" Hawk asked.

"I don't know what they did, but it's like every camera in a five-mile radius was turned off for five minutes. I'm trying to recreate their exit, but it'll take me forever to distill the possibilities. And I'm afraid by then it'll be far too late."

"Is there any other way you can figure out where they're going?" Hawk asked.

"If I look at the time just before they left, I might be able to figure out something," she said. "But that's only if they slipped up and made a mistake. In the midst of that kind of chaos, it is possible."

"Okay, just do whatever you think will help you find them," Hawk said. "But before you disappear into all those images, do you know where Black is?"

"Talk to Blunt," she said.

A few seconds later, Blunt came on the coms. "What is it, Hawk?"

"I need Black. Where is he? I thought he was supposed to be patrolling the grounds and looking for anything even remotely suspicious."

"Well, he just got here," Blunt said. "And he's got some explaining to do."

"He's at the Phoenix Foundation? Right now?"

"He walked in a few minutes ago—with his sister."

"What's he doing with his sister?" Hawk asked. "This is one of our most important missions ever and he's decided that now he needs more family time?"

"It's a long story, but apparently the short version is that she was being held against her will."

"By who?"

"Not sure yet. He promised to tell me everything soon, but in the meantime, I'm just going to trust him."

"You know I like Black, but that makes me a little wary of what he's been doing. I'd never—"

"Yeah, I wouldn't recommend finishing that sentence," Blunt said. "If you were in his situation, who knows what you would or wouldn't do?"

"But I certainly would have a conversation with someone about it before I did it."

"You would? I wouldn't count on that."

Hawk sighed. "Well, maybe a few times I decided to do what I wanted to do and somehow avoided the crushing consequences, but there were good reasons for what I did every single time."

"In your opinion," Blunt said.

"In everybody's opinion. People understood that. It's not like I was some renegade, who threw caution to the wind and ignored the sage advice of some more elderly people in my life. I was always listening."

"Our perceptions of our own lives often vary quite differently from reality."

"What exactly are you trying to say?"

"You're a damn good operative, Hawk, but self-analysis and introspection may not be your greatest qualities. However, I prefer right now that you stick to being a great agent and find Young. Alex is tracking your location now and will send Black to you."

"Roger that. Let me know when you have a general direction to start looking."

Hawk reached his car and slid into the front seat. Turning the key in the ignition, the car roared to life. He peeled out of the parking deck and sped onto the streets.

"Talk to me, Alex," Hawk said over his coms. "I'm in the car and ready to go somewhere."

"I'm looking," she said. "The local authorities are coordinating with the FBI and have set up a five-mile perimeter around Capitol Hill."

"At least you know where to look."

"Yeah, but what kind of location are we looking for? That's the million dollar question I can't answer right now."

"I'd start with warehouses," Hawk said. "Maybe search for ones on the leasing market. That's how I'd find an open space if I were in her position."

Hawk heard Alex's fingers tapping furiously on her keyboard followed by a sigh.

"What is it?" Hawk asked.

"Good idea, but that's narrowed it down to just under a hundred possibilities."

"Can you map those? Maybe even see if there was any activity at those locations in the past twenty minutes? Just a suggestion."

"It's a great one, but it'll take me some time."

"Fine," Hawk said. "Why don't you send me the closest ones, and I'll start to visit a few myself."

"I'm texting you a short list now."

* * *

BLUNT PACED around the office, gnawing on his cigar and mumbling to himself. Evana Bahar had made a brazen attack during the middle of the State of the Union address and had thrown the capitol into complete chaos. Even the safe distance they were away from the epicenter, he could hear emergency vehicle sirens wailing into the night.

"Did Hawk have any useful ideas?" he asked.

"I'm narrowing down potential locations but trying to figure out a quicker way to do this. To be honest, I'm not sure how helpful this will be. But until

I have another lead, this is about as good as it gets."

Blunt turned his focus toward the television on the far wall where a reporter was giving a live report. He turned up the volume to hear what she was saying.

In the background, people scurried in all directions, fleeing the building. She stressed that there was no point person yet who was communicating with the press or the public about what action officials were taking to get the president back. Then the picture started to flit in and out as if there was some type of magnetic interference. After a few seconds, the picture dissolved to black.

"Hmm. That's weird."

Then Evana Bahar appeared on the screen, her face just a couple of feet from the camera.

"Good evening, Americans," she began. "It would be a shame that if in a country proud of its so-called freedom you wouldn't get to see the trial of your president and hear him answer for all the crimes he's committed against you and other nations."

She paced around Young, who was tied to a chair and gagged. With a smug grin on her face, she stopped to his right and ran the back of her hand across his cheek.

"America, the land of opportunity—if you're handsome enough. Who cares what your leaders do with their power as long as it's an attractive person wielding it over you. The American people don't even care about platform issues as much as its leaders think. They'll swing from one party's leader to the next just as long as he—or, maybe one day, she—looks the part."

Young grimaced as she continued speaking. At one point, the camera zoomed in on him, showing just how uncomfortable and terrified he was. He squirmed, fighting against the ropes that secured him to his seat.

Upon noticing Young's blatant resistance, Evana rolled her eyes and resumed walking around him.

"Now, let's cut to the chase, President Young. I'm sure the American people would be keenly interested in how you're invading their privacy, a right so many people here hold dear."

Blunt kicked over a nearby chair. "Turn it off. I can't stand to watch her do this him. She's going to torture him and kill him unless we can do something about it. Where are you at on identifying their location?"

Alex continued typing, refusing to look up. "I'm still comparing all the locations with the pictures just before all the cameras went dark and the most recent satellite images.

"What I don't understand is if Al Fatihin has the technology to disrupt all these closed-circuit cameras, why are they all working again?" Blunt asked.

"That's a good question. The only working theory I can offer on that is if they were using some type of magnetic source strong enough to affect all these cameras, they may not have the energy source required to keep it constant. However, for their purposes, it was plenty effective. We weren't able to follow them anywhere."

Alex glanced up at the television, and her mouth fell agape. Blunt saw her and slowly turned to look with her, even though he didn't want to.

The scene depicted made him so angry that he clenched his fists and started shaking with rage. "I wish I could put her down myself."

Alex nodded. "You and me both."

Young was still tied up, but Evana had placed electrode pads all over his body. She held up a small device with a button, pressing it intermittently and laughing maniacally as Young shook and convulsed.

Blunt turned away. "Is there any way you can track that feed? There has to be some way to figure out where they are."

"Pinpointing the location of that stream source would take quite a while, and I'm not sure we have that much time."

Blunt glanced back at the television and saw Young enduring longer stretches of Evana's torture device.

"You're right," Blunt said. "We don't have much time at all."

CHAPTER 18

A'ISHA STOOD ALONE in the Capitol Building, where just an hour earlier she was on stage, smiling and basking in the warmth of American kindness and generosity. But all of that goodwill had vanished with the information that Evana Bahar had filled her prosthetic leg with explosives. At least, that was the story. No one had bothered to check if that was true.

She sat down on the end of the stage and was about to unlatch her leg when she felt something crinkle in her pocket.

That's odd. I don't remember having anything in my pocket.

Tucked inside her dress pocket was a small envelope addressed to her. She tore it open and read a letter.

Dear A'isha,
I know you're probably scared right now and wondering what's happening to you. Just

know it is all for the best and that your mother loves you very much.

Forever yours,

Jahedah

P.S. Whatever you do, don't remove your leg.

A'isha was confused. Her mother's notes were always warm and tender. And she never called herself Jahedah. It was always al'umu. But using her first name seemed rather odd. For a moment, A'isha wondered if her mother even wrote the note, though a quick inspection of the handwriting confirmed that the message was indeed penned by Jahedah.

Adding to A'isha's confusion was the fact that she didn't know where to go. She refolded the note and shoved it back into her pocket before breaking down and heaving. Hot tears streaked down her face, which she buried in her hands. What difference did a leg make if she was going to be treated like a pariah or left to die in isolation?

After a few minutes, she stopped crying and started to study her leg more closely. She thought the nurse who helped her earlier in the day had done something to the leg since it was noticeably heavier. When A'isha had complained about the weight, the nurse told her that it would help her strengthen her muscles and it'd only be necessary for a few days.

But now A'isha knew that was all a lie. Whoever the woman was, she had somehow inserted a bomb inside the prosthetic.

She hiked up her skirt and peered at the bindings. Anxious to remove it, she searched for the latches when she read a message scrawled in English and Arabic on a piece of tape near the latch. It read: "Do not remove under any circumstances."

A'isha stopped, fearful of what might happen if she forged ahead and tried to take it off.

"That was a smart move," said a man in Arabic from across the room.

She glanced around in an attempt to find his location. When she looked forward again, he was standing in front of her.

"A'isha, my name is Agent Nelson. I've been asked to give you a ride and get you to safety."

She eyed him closely, narrowing her eyes. "How do I know you are who you say you are?"

He reached into his pocket and produced an identification badge that he gave her. While she had no idea what a CIA official's badge looked like, she noticed a sticker in the center that changed colors when she rotated it beneath the bright overhead lights. And the image on the card matched what he looked like. She handed it back to him.

"Where do you want to take me?" she asked.

"Some place safe where you won't be used like a pawn again."

"Will I be able to take this leg off?"

He shrugged. "If you'd like; that's up to you. I thought you were excited about receiving such an incredible piece of technology."

She sighed. "I'll forever remember what happened here tonight whenever I put it on in the future."

"Look, we all suffer in our lives, but we move on—at least, we should. You're young, and I have no doubt that you'll be able to move on, probably much sooner than you think you can right now."

A'isha stood, and her eyes met Nelson's. "I'm ready to go. Please take me some place safe."

"Good. We need to hurry and get far away from here."

"Why? What could happen?"

Nelson took her hand and helped her down the steps before striding up the aisle to the exit. "I'll explain everything later. We don't have any time to waste."

A'isha came to an abrupt halt, stamping her foot as she did. "I'm not going anywhere until you tell me why we need to hurry and why we need to get so far away from here."

Nelson sighed. "The quick story is that we're in

danger right now due to the way that bomb in your leg can be detonated. If we're in range of a cell phone tower, we're in danger, so I need to get you far away from here."

"Then where are we going?"

"We're going to the train station. We first need to disappear from the area, and then I'm going to drive you up into the Catskill Mountains in New York where nobody will find us unless we want to be found."

A'isha resumed her pace, passing Nelson, who was standing still and shaking his head.

"You're quite a firecracker," Nelson said.

"A what?"

"Never mind," he said. "Let's just keep going."

A'isha charged ahead, fighting back tears. Despite the kindness of Agent Nelson, she was still grappling with swirling emotions, ranging from rage to gratefulness and terror to courage.

CHAPTER 19

HAWK SKIDDED TO A STOP at the curb and reached across the passenger seat to fling open the door. After Black hustled over to the car, he jumped inside. Checking the rearview mirror, Hawk sped off.

"Where have you been?" Hawk asked, dispensing with pleasantries. "We needed your help tonight."

"You've got it now," Black said. "But I'm not a magician. I can't change the past."

"You're not answering my question."

Hawk gave Black a sideways glance as the car roared through an intersection.

"It's a long story and—"

"And I already know the shortened version. But I want to hear what you were doing with your sister. Why tonight of all nights?"

"Can we just focus on finding Young right now? I'll tell you everything later."

"No," Hawk said, narrowing his eyes as he shot a quick look again at Black. "This is a matter of trust.

And if I can't trust you right now, this isn't going to work."

"Fine," Black said. "Fortner kidnapped my sister and was holding her hostage."

"He was in Chile, wasn't he?"

Black nodded.

Hawk slammed the steering wheel with his fist. "I knew it. That intel was solid, and I was struggling to believe we had missed it so badly."

Black explained the full story to Hawk as they drove from location to location in search of the warehouse where Evana Bahar and her cell were broadcasting their torture of President Young. At times, Black's story seemed almost unbelievable, but Hawk tried to take Blunt's advice and keep an open mind.

Hawk jerked the wheel to the right as the car fishtailed on the snow-slick surface. Every few minutes, the precipitation's intensity seemed to increase.

As Black continued sharing his side of the events, Hawk attempted to put himself in that same scenario. If he had a sister in danger at the hands of a madman, Hawk concluded he probably would've done the same thing. Once Black finished, Hawk patted his partner on the back.

"How's your sister doing?" Hawk asked.

"She's pretty shaken up, not to mention the fact that she now knows I'm a secret government operative. That was all news to her."

Hawk chuckled as he rolled into the parking lot of another potential place Young was being held. "She'll probably never look at you the same again, will she?"

"I highly doubt it—and I'll bet that she'll have a hard time trusting any strangers in the future."

"Join the club," Hawk said with a laugh. "We're partners, and this whole conversation started because I was having a difficult time trusting you. Even those closest to us can make us hold everyone suspect. And that's not necessarily a bad thing."

"Are we good now?" Black asked.

Hawk reached over gave Black a fist bump. "We're good now, and I'm sorry for being so hard on you about this. You've gotta protect your family, something I don't have anymore."

"You've got Alex."

"Of course, but I'm talking about your blood kin, the people who've been there with you and for you your entire life. I'm referring to the brothers, sisters, parents, cousins, aunts, uncles—everyone who saw you grow up and know the best and worst sides of you. When you lose that, it's like you lose a little piece of yourself. I lost that a long time ago, and in some ways, I never really had it."

"You have Blunt."

Hawk nodded. "And he's the reason I ever considered this job in the first place. In a field riddled with deceit, you need a constant, a rock, someone you can count on."

"That's what Laura is for me. And although I'm not sure it'll be like this in the future, any time I visit her, I forget about this work for a few hours and just relax."

Hawk turned off the engine. "Well, let's go check out this facility and see if it's what we're looking for."

Both agents stealthily stepped out of the vehicle and crept around the corner of the building, weapons drawn. They peered inside, and it seemed completely empty.

"There's nothing in here from what I can see," Black said.

"Me either, but I want to check one more thing."

Hawk hustled around the side of the building, looking for any sign that Al Fatihin was utilizing the structure. He aimed his flashlight inside the stark facility, illuminating the reception area. There wasn't as much as a piece of paper strewn on the floor. He then went around to the other side and found the power breaker off and padlocked in place.

"See anything?" Black asked as he hustled after Hawk.

"Not a damn thing," Hawk said as he pointed at the power box. "This thing is locked shut and off.

There's no way they could be utilizing this place."

"So now what?" Black asked. "Got any great ideas pinging around in that head of yours?"

"We just keep marching down the list," Hawk said.

They raced back to the car, and Hawk contacted Alex via the coms.

"We just struck out again," Hawk said. "We're not finding anything. Have you been able to narrow things down at all for us?"

"Well, I can rule out a few places. I'm texting you a list that you can eliminate from your search, but unfortunately, we just have to keep looking. However, we need to move quickly."

"Why? Any update on Young?"

"Evana is getting more brutal by the minute. Hawk, I'm worried he might not survive much more of this."

"What about A'isha?" Hawk asked.

"She's gone," Alex said.

"What do you mean she's gone?"

"Blunt was wondering the same thing, so I tapped into the capitol's security feed. And she's not in the chamber."

"Did law enforcement get her out of there?" Hawk asked.

"That's all I can figure right now. I doubt she decided to start wandering the streets of Washington on her own."

"See what you can find out, okay?"

Alex sighed. "I'm not sure that's a top priority right now."

"Then call someone who can help you. We need to find her before Evana tries to use the girl again."

Hawk's phone buzzed.

"You gonna get that?" Black asked.

Hawk nodded. "I've got another call coming in, Alex. Just keep this channel open in case we need you."

"Roger that," she said.

Hawk answered his cell.

"Mr. Hawk, did I catch you at a bad time?" a man asked. Hawk recognized the voice right away.

"General Fortner, to what do I owe the pleasure of this call?"

"I couldn't reach your colleague, but I wanted to call and thank him for leading us straight to your offices. I half expected Black to attempt to free his sister. And thanks to my brilliant foresight, I inserted a tracker in her. And now I know exactly where she is, not to mention where Alex and J.D. are hiding out. As we speak, our agents are surrounding the Phoenix Foundation. And I'm going to have to ask you two to stand down in your search for Evana Bahar."

Hawk didn't say a word. He simply hung up and tried to reach Alex through the coms, but she wasn't answering.

CHAPTER 20

ALEX LOOKED AT HER PHONE, which was buzzing with a notification from the Phoenix Foundation's security system. She furrowed her brow and scanned the room for Blunt. His cane was still resting against the wall in the corner where he'd left it when he came in.

"Blunt," she called. "Are you still here?"

"Yeah," he answered. "I'm across the hall with Laura."

She hopped up from her desk and walked to the adjacent room where they were.

"She said she was hungry, so I went to get her something to eat," Blunt said.

"Did you leave the office?"

"No. Why?"

"I got an alert letting me know that there's some activity outside."

Blunt scowled. "Let me have a look."

They both returned to Alex's office and called up

the security cameras. They were all black.

"Something's wrong," Blunt said.

Alex reached inside her desk and pulled out her gun. "We need to move."

"It's Laura," Blunt said. "They must've put a tracker in her."

Alex hustled downstairs and grabbed a security wand, careful not to turn on any lights. She noticed the glint of a headlamp outside.

Racing back up the steps, she waved the wand around Laura.

"What's happening now?" she asked.

"Just stay calm, but I think Fortner's people put a tracker in you and they're coming for you now," Alex said.

The wand beeped as Alex hovered it over Laura's forearm. Alex snatched a knife out of her pocket.

"This is going to hurt a little, but I have to get this out of here."

Laura nodded and closed her eyes. Without hesitating, Alex jammed the blade into Laura's skin and quickly dug out the tracker. Blunt raised up to smash it, but Alex grabbed his wrist before he did.

"What are you doing?" Blunt said. "We need to end this transmission before we head to the panic room."

"We can use this to divert them away from here."

"And how do you expect to do that?"

Alex rummaged through her desk drawer. "Apply some pressure to Laura's arm with this rag while I look for something." Moments later, she pulled out a box.

"What's that?" Blunt asked as he followed Alex's directive to assist Laura.

"When Hawk was in Pakistan, he mentioned that he wanted a drone," Alex said. "So he's got a birthday coming up and I thought I would surprise him with one."

"Brilliant idea," he said.

"I'm not sure I follow what's happening," Laura said.

"Watch," Alex said as she took a piece of tape and fastened the tracker to the drone.

She paused for a moment, wanting to create a diversion before unleashing the drone. After grabbing her keys, she pressed the panic button, setting off the alarm from her car. With all the agents hopefully wondering what was going on, she eased open a window and released the stealth drone outside.

Despite the successful launch of the diversion, she grabbed her laptop and two others before urging Blunt to retreat to the panic room. He retrieved his cane and hobbled down the steps, well behind Alex and Laura.

"Come on, come on," she called. "From what I

can see outside, several operatives are following the tracker, but a couple other agents are still just outside the front door. You need to get a move on."

"I'm going as fast as I can, Alex."

As he was making his way down to the main level, the glass to the front door shattered, splintering into hundreds of pieces as it hit the ground. A smoke grenade followed, quickly filling the room.

Alex took up a position against the wall and waited. Just as Blunt reached the last step, two hostiles emerged from the smoke with their weapons trained forward. Alex hit the first man in the head before blasting the other man with two shots in the chest. They both crumpled.

"Hurry," Alex said, reaching out her hand to assist Blunt. Once she took hold of him, they turned the corner and disappeared into the panic room.

Satisfied that they were out of harm's way despite the presence of the enemy combatants just outside, she collapsed against the wall and opened up her computers to resume her work. She reinserted her earbud and adjusted it.

"Alex, Alex. Can you hear me?" Hawk asked.

"Yeah, I'm here," she said. "We're dealing with some hostiles here at the headquarters."

"What's going on?"

"Apparently, they put a tracker in Laura and

found us. We're safe now, holed up in the panic room. I don't think they'll be able to get in here before Blunt calls in a few favors and summons people over here to help us out, but I've fallen behind on eliminating some of these possible locations."

"We're coming back."

"No," she said. "Stay out there. We can handle this. You need to find Young."

"Is Evana still broadcasting?" Hawk asked.

"I haven't had a chance to look for a while now. Just give me a few minutes to get everything back up online and working again. I'll update you then."

"Okay, but you better not hesitate to call us if you feel like you're in serious danger. I'll ditch this assignment for you in a flash."

"You know I can handle myself. Now, keep looking."

Hawk said something, but his words became a garbled mess due to static and other interferences. Outside, gunfire erupted. Shots echoed down the hall and included prolonged periods of silence before the firing started up again.

"They're going to kill us, aren't they?" Laura asked, eyes wide with terror.

Blunt shook his head resolutely. "You will live, but they'll definitely kill me. You and Alex can be used to persuade your loved ones, but I'm worthless to their agenda. I'm just a rock in their shoe they'd like to remove sooner rather than later."

"Maybe they'll take the people you love," Laura said.

"I love everyone on this team and my country," Blunt said. "It keeps my life simple and straightforward, just how I like it."

A flurry of shots sounded like they were being fired at the entry panel next to the door. Blunt had gone to painstaking lengths to disguise the panel while designing the facility. There weren't even any seams around the door, but someone had figured it out and was trying to get in.

"Get behind me," Alex said to Laura, who promptly obeyed.

Blunt sat on a chair right in front of the door, holding his cane loosely. Alex stood, her gun trained on the opening, ready to pump the person full of every bullet in her chamber.

After a few more attempts at the control panel, the lock released and the door slid open.

Smoke poured into the room and Alex steadied her hands as she braced for a shootout.

But before she could fire her weapon, she felt a burning sensation in her neck. Everything around her went dark as she collapsed.

CHAPTER 21

EVANA BAHAR PLODDED ACROSS the room to a table in the corner where she studied a number of items strewn across it. After a moment, she selected a cropping stick and placed it behind her back. President Young watched the entire scene unfold with keen interest as he wondered how she intended to torture him with this new device.

He closed his eyes, squeezing them shut. They were already burning, and he was trying to do whatever he could to avoid another round of pain. While there wasn't much he could do with his hands tied behind his back, he thought that maybe the tears could keep his eyes clear and free. In the end, it was a good idea that only managed to deliver a couple seconds of relief before the fiery sensation returned.

Her boots clicked against the concrete floor as she walked up to the camera and tapped on it.

"Hello, America," she said. "Have you had enough of your president's lies yet? Shouldn't he pay for what he's done to this country? Tonight, he tried to shovel a steam pile of garbage onto you— otherwise known as propaganda—and expected you to lap it up. But the truth is so far from what he said tonight that it's laughable. He's either severely disconnected from reality or he has no conscience and doesn't care that he's lying to you. Frankly, I find both of these options disturbing."

Young writhed and moaned, twisting and turning against the ropes tethering him to the chair. Despite the futility of the act, he didn't want the American people's final image of him to be a spineless leader going down without putting up a fight.

"Just look at him," Evana said, nodding across the room behind her. "He's so weak and pathetic. He knows that his judgment day is nigh, and he doesn't want to face the consequences. But we all must face consequences, even our leaders—especially the leaders who amass power through murdering innocent people."

Even while gagged, Young growled and shook his head back and forth. There was nothing dignified about his actions, but he wasn't interested in looking like a politician. He just wanted to be remembered as a fighter.

"Now, what's funny is the fact that President Young actually does negotiate with terrorists," she said with a faint grin. "Just a few weeks ago, I was able to get him to return one of my top bomb makers just so he could have back some secret agent who supposedly doesn't even exist. I knew that the line about negotiating with terrorists was something almost all presidents say just to talk tough, acting as if that's the red line they won't cross. But red lines are drawn more to placate political bases rather than to enforce strict boundaries for dealing with terrorists. If terrorists kidnapped a senator's child, you can be sure that money or other valuable commodities would exchange hands. How do I know that? Because I've done it before, all outside the bright lights of your news cameras."

"That's a lie," shouted Young in the background.

The camera panned over to him. He'd twisted back and forth until he had worked the gag out of his mouth. She rushed over toward him.

"This is all propaganda," Young said as he rocked back and forth. "Don't do anything to get me out of here. I—"

Evana chuckled. "Isn't he charming to the end, still peddling his lies and trusting that you'll believe his stories without questioning them? Well, this ends tonight, and you're all going to have a front-row view."

She spun around, turning her back on the camera, which followed her across the room to Young.

He continued to shout at her, refuting everything she said. With a smirk, she shook her head as she stared down at him.

"It's too late, Mr. President. Nobody will buy your pack of lies anymore."

With that statement, she drew back her stick and struck him repeatedly in the head until he fell unconscious.

* * *

EVANA BAHAR SMACKED Young's face several times, checking to see if he was out. She felt his neck for a pulse.

"Not to worry," she said, looking directly at the camera. "He's still alive. I wouldn't let him get off that easily."

She took a deep breath and smiled wide. Reveling in her moment of fame, she knew this would surely make her immortal. History books the world over would tell of the time an American president was taken hostage, judged, and punished for his criminal behavior toward the rest of the world. Her cousin, Karif Fazil, had laid out a blueprint for how to put on a show and exact retribution from a world leader. But Fazil's plan hadn't taken every detail into account, primarily Brady Hawk and his creativity when it came to outwitting his foes. Evana was convinced she would build on Fazil's idea and take it to the dramatic conclusion that he couldn't produce. However, he didn't have the kind of help she had.

Out of the blue one day, an Obsidian representative showed up at one of her hideouts. The man claimed to be unarmed and said he needed to talk with her—and if she tried to run, she and her organization would be obliterated. It was the kind of offer she couldn't refuse, but not because of the threat. Despite the predatory way she was approached, she saw a genuine opportunity for the kind of partnership that could wreak havoc on the world— and the kind of assistance she needed to pull off her public hanging of President Young.

She picked up her phone and dialed a number. "Kill the security cameras. We need to go out again."

CHAPTER 22

HAWK AND BLACK CONTINUED racing from one warehouse on the list to another, trying to follow the game plan Alex laid out for them. But with so many possibilities in the area and the slow pace at which the pair of Phoenix Foundation operatives were eliminating them, Hawk grew frustrated. Outside of a lucky break, he realized there was no way to find President Young before Evana Bahar did her worst to him.

"There has to be another way to go about this," Hawk said as they hustled back to the car after crossing another property off the list.

"It'd be a helluva lot easier if Alex could just track that live stream Evana is pumping onto the internet," Black said. "Then we might actually have time to figure out how we're going to stop Al Fatihin once we get there."

"Well, she said that if there's one thing that terrorist organization does well, it's the internet security. She told me it's one of the most advanced systems she's ever tried to crack over the last five years. And coming from her, that's saying something."

"How long would it take?" Black asked. "It can't be any longer than it's going to take for us to ferret these people out by going literally door to door."

"She says it would—and I tend to trust her on matters like this."

Hawk sighed. "Outside of Alex getting any more help on this one, I think this is how we have to do it. But like you, I'm not happy about this, mostly because I think we're headed for a dead end. And I mean that in a very literal sense."

"Try to get Alex back on the coms," Black said. "We should've heard from her by now."

Hawk attempted to connect with her over the coms. After several tries, there was no response.

"Maybe they went down with all that fighting," Black suggested. "You should see if you can reach her on your phone."

Hawk unlocked his cell phone and was about to start dialing when something flashed on the screen that arrested his attention. He gasped as his eyes widened.

"What is it?" Black asked.

"They're on the move again," Hawk said, shaking his head in disbelief. "This might all be for naught."

"How do you know they're moving?"

"There's an alert from two minutes ago that says Al Fatihin has ended its feed but promised—and I quote—'more fireworks to come'."

Black shook his head. "If that's not cryptic, I don't know what is."

"Cryptic or not, it means all the time we spent eliminating potential locations has just been rendered meaningless," Hawk said. "If they're on the move now, they could wind up at a place we've already checked. And by the time we circled back around to it, we'd be too late."

"Maybe Alex can come up with some other way to identify Al Fatihin's location in Washington using some type of algorithm or something."

Hawk chuckled. "Is that how you think every problem should be solved by those brilliant computer whizzes?"

Black shrugged. "Why not? That's what they do, isn't it?"

"They don't sit around all day and write algorithms. And even if they did, putting one together is incredibly challenging. I observed that first-hand as a spouse who knows just how difficult it can be to survive on your own for two straight months while your partner is off working on a project like this one."

"So, I'm taking that as a hard no," Black said. "Tell me if I'm misreading you here."

"You're getting the message loud and clear," Hawk said. "She wouldn't have time to create any program like that. Evana Bahar is not going to make it easy on us; that's already quite certain.

"Call her phone and see if things have changed," Black said.

Hawk dialed Alex's number, but he went straight to voicemail. He tried several times. But still nothing.

"No, no. This can't be," Hawk muttered.

"No answer?" Black asked.

Hawk shook his head.

"We need to get to headquarters real quick and make sure everyone is okay," Black said.

"If we do that, we're going to lose valuable time that we need to catch Evana and the other Al Fatihin agents."

"But Alex actually knows how to help us. Without her, we're looking for a needle in a haystack."

Hawk's phone buzzed, and he stared at his screen before groaning.

"Who is it?" Black asked.

"It's my—It's Thomas Colton."

"He's calling right now? What does he want?" Black asked.

"I don't know, but it can't be good," Hawk said before answering.

"Son—I mean, Brady—I know you're probably

really busy right now and don't have much time to talk, but there's something I need to tell you."

"What's so urgent?" Hawk asked.

"I know how the terrorists are moving around in the city without getting caught," Colton said.

"What did you create this time?"

"The Electron 451—the most powerful portable electromagnetic field device ever built. We designed it so the military could knock out an enemy's ability to track them in the field during close-range battles. We were transporting several of them last week, and the best we can figure is that one was stolen as we were moving them across the country."

"For all your high-tech development, you really need to get a better security system. Between things getting stolen and the weapons resold on the black market, I'm starting to think we'd be better off without Colton Industries."

"Look, I know that's how it's seemed lately, but this is a much-needed weapon in today's warfare."

Hawk groaned. "And now Al Fatihin has it— along with the president."

"Yeah, but there's a way to pinpoint its location that they wouldn't necessarily know about," Colton said. "While Al Fatihin may think they've gotten away with racing around the city in darkness, the Electro 451 creates a perfect five-mile radius. If you can determine the perimeter, you should be able to figure out where it was being utilized."

"But that's not a guarantee that they will be there."

"I know, but it's a starting point. Anything to help."

"Thanks for letting me know," Hawk said. "I'll call you if we have any other questions about this."

Hawk hung up and looked at Black. "We need Alex's help right now."

As they roared across the city toward the Phoenix Foundation offices, Black kept trying Alex's phone periodically. Meanwhile, Hawk explained what Colton had told him about the Electro 451 and how it worked.

Upon arriving at the Phoenix Foundation offices, Hawk swiped his security badge and waited for the underground parking garage gate to open. He looked around and noticed the outside of the building looked like a war zone with shattered glass and munitions casings strewn all over.

"What happened here?" Hawk asked.

Black shook his head. "This isn't good."

Hawk entered the garage and noticed Alex's car was still here, along with Blunt's and a couple of others that were familiar.

Accessing the elevator, Hawk and Black rode up

in silence. Hawk was already thinking the worst, and he could read the same concern on Black's face. When the doors finally opened, the pair of agents marched into a hazy hallway where the smell of gunpowder hung in the air.

Hawk stepped over several bodies strewn across the floor. He didn't recognize any of them, though he noted they were all wearing dark-blue uniforms.

"Alex! Blunt! Laura! Talk to me. Where are you guys?" Hawk called.

With his weapon drawn, he hustled down the hallway to the panic room. The access panel had been destroyed, and the door was wide open.

"Alex said they were all in the panic room," Hawk said before kicking one of the chairs across the room.

"They couldn't be all that far away. We'll find them, Hawk."

They stepped back into the hallway. Hawk knelt next to one of the dead attackers.

"Someone's gonna pay for this," Hawk said.

CHAPTER 23

ALEX RUBBED HER NECK as she opened her eyes and surveyed the room. She was lying on a couch in an office. Shelves loaded with reference books lined the back wall while a desk with a computer and chair was on the opposite side. There was a minimalist design to the space, something she figured was quite intentional.

As she sat up and eased her feet onto the floor, she winced. However, she was surprised not to find herself in chains. Her initial instinct was to run, but she didn't sense danger, which seemed awkward given the circumstances.

Alex buried her head in her hands and stayed that way until she heard a voice coming from the hallway.

"You're safe now," a man said.

She looked up and saw CIA Deputy Director Randy Wood leaning against the doorjamb.

"Wha—what happened? You guys shot me?" she asked.

"Sedated you, actually," Wood said. "There was so much chaos in the hallway at the time, our team leader thought it would be the best way to get everyone to safety."

"But I thought—" she stopped and sighed. "Someone was attacking us, right? I wasn't imagining that, was I?"

"No, you were under siege," Wood said. "We were sending a team over to pick you up anyway because we thought the facility had been compromised."

"Based on what?"

"Based on some chatter we picked up."

"From Al Fatihin?"

Wood shook his head. "There's another far more dangerous group we've been monitoring—and only a handful of my most trusted agents know about it."

"Obsidian?"

He nodded. "We're still trying to figure out who's involved, how they're connected, and what their end game is. I'm thinking you might know something."

"You should talk to Blunt about that."

"I intend to once he wakes up. But honestly, that's not why you're here. We need your help to find these bastards and get the president back."

Alex nodded subtly. "Get me some water and some aspirin to help with the headache, and point me to a computer terminal."

"Just follow me." Wood gestured toward the hallway.

Alex wanted to call Hawk and let him know that she was okay, but she couldn't. Not with everything that was going on.

As they hustled toward the department of analysts, Alex tried to suppress the painful memories of the last time she was here. She was toting a box of all her office possessions and hanging her head as colleagues shot glances at her and whispered to one another. The walk of shame shook her confidence and made her seem toxic to her former co-workers. Instead of receiving calls to check on her, most of them let her know that they would not be communicating with her anymore. While she had only been fired, the entire episode felt like a funeral—and it was her own.

"He's gone now," Wood said as he turned and looked at Alex.

"Who?"

"Your old boss. He was fired six months ago. And I'd hire you back in a heartbeat if I could pry you away from Blunt. I know that'll never happen, but if you ever want a new challenge—"

She forced a smile. "I appreciate the gesture, sir. I'm not sure I'll ever get over what happened here."

"I understand, but I just thought you'd like to know that the current leadership here at the agency doesn't feel the way the old one did regarding your skillset."

"That's kind of you to say."

Wood stopped in front of the entrance to the analyst area and held the door open for Alex, ushering her inside.

"I'll get you set up over here," he said.

Alex's phone buzzed in her pocket. She scanned the message from Hawk. When she finished reading it, she sat down in her chair and typed a response.

"Do you need someone to catch you up to speed on where everything is?" Wood asked as he leaned on the desk.

She shot him a sideways glance. "I've spent so much time in this system over the past couple of years, it's like I never left."

Wood nodded. "Let me know if you need anything else."

"Just that water and aspirin."

She hammered away on the keyboard for a few seconds to get herself set up before calling Hawk.

"Where are you?" she asked in a hushed tone.

"Oh, thank God you're okay," Hawk said. "We're at the headquarters now, and this place looks like a war zone. Where are you?"

"I'm at Langley."

"Langley? What are you doing there? And why did it take so long for you to return my calls? I've been worried sick about you."

"I can explain everything later, but Randy Wood just set me up with a terminal and full access to the CIA's servers. So, I'm catching up on what's going on. We need to find the president. But while I'm working, tell me more about this Electro 451."

Hawk explained how it worked and gave Alex all the parameters she needed to start her search.

"This might take me a few minutes, but I should be able to narrow this down pretty quickly, especially if everything goes out again."

"That's the thing," Hawk said. "I think everything just came back online."

After a couple minutes, she clapped her hands together and then pumped her fists.

"Gotcha," she yelled.

Wood ran over to her. "What'd you find?"

"Al Fatihin was using this new technology from Colton Industries that allowed them to interfere with closed-circuit television feeds. According to Colton, the device creates a five-mile radius, allowing us to identify its location with a few waypoints."

"So you have the address?"

She nodded.

"Give it to me, and I'll get a team over there right away."

"That'd take too long," she said. "But Hawk and Black are only a mile away."

"Let me at least send backup."

Alex scribbled down the address on a piece of paper and handed it to Wood.

"Excellent," Wood said. "I'll send a team there now. But I'm coming right back. I want a real-time report on what they find."

* * *

HAWK AND BLACK ROARED toward the location of the warehouse Alex had identified. They swerved in and out of traffic, cutting off several vehicles and narrowly missing another.

As Hawk neared the facility, he killed his lights and slowed down.

"I don't see any movement," he said. "Do you?"

"Nothing," Black said. "Are you sure this is the right address?"

Hawk checked his phone. "Yep, this is the one Alex texted me."

"Let's go have a look."

After putting in their coms, Hawk and Black drew their weapons and crept toward the edge of the building. There was a large sign on the window with all the contact details for leasing. Hawk yanked the door handle, and it was locked.

"Let's go around the side," he said.

The facility was two stories and constructed of cinder blocks with very few windows.

"Alex, what business was in here before it went vacant?" Hawk asked over the coms.

"It manufactured boat engine parts for a couple different companies."

"Can you look at the schematics and tell me what we'd be heading into here?" Hawk asked.

"Just give me a second."

Alex's fingers flew over the keyboard as she dug up the records on file. "Okay, got it. There are just a couple of offices on the second floor, which only extends about fifty feet back. Then the rest of the space is just a giant two-story warehouse."

"I don't see a single light anywhere."

"Me either," Black said.

Hawk nodded at Black. "We're going in for a closer look."

Black found a door on the backside that was padlocked. He shot it off and then picked the lock. Hawk followed Black inside as they scoped out the empty space.

"There's not even a stray bolt in here," Hawk said. "This place is as clean as a whistle. Going upstairs now."

They found a stairwell near the front and slowly ascended, moving stealthily. Hawk didn't hear anything. They glided from room to room, clearing each one with precision. In less than a minute, they determined the building was devoid of any people.

"There's nothing here," Hawk said. "Are you sure this is the place?"

"According to my calculations, there isn't another facility they could've used in the general vicinity," Alex said. "That has to be it."

"Well, it's another dead end."

Hawk froze when he heard the sound of metal clanging against the concrete floor.

"Someone's here," Black said.

They raced downstairs, guns trained straight ahead. When they tore through the door leading to the open area, they found a man lugging a box as he sprinted toward the door.

"Hold it right there," Hawk said.

The man didn't even look back, continuing his getaway. Hawk and Black dashed after the man, catching him after about fifty meters in the parking lot. Tackled by Hawk, the man squirmed as he tried to escape, but Black trained his gun on the man's head, ending any more struggling.

"Who are you, and what are you doing here?" Hawk asked.

"Don't hurt me, please," said the wiry man. He appeared to be in his mid-twenties. Hawk could barely see the man's eyes as his long brown hair was strewn across his face.

"I'm not making any promises," Hawk said with a growl. "Now answer the question."

"Okay, okay. I just answered this ad I found online, and it was an easy five hundred bucks. All I had to do was turn on this machine for a few minutes at a couple locations whenever I got a phone call from this lady. I don't even think it does anything. Maybe this is some kind of prank. I don't know. But it's five hundred bucks, man."

"Yeah, well, you're aiding and abetting terrorists," Hawk said. "Give me your phone."

"It's not going to help you," the man said. "There's no number when she calls me. It's all blocked."

"Just give it to me," Hawk demanded, holding out his hand.

"What are you going to do with it? It cost me more than I'm making on this job."

Hawk glared at him. "You better be thankful I'm not carting your ass to prison. Now, I'm not going to ask again."

"Fine," the man said as he slapped the phone into Hawk's hand.

Hawk released the man. "Alex, are you still with us?"

"Yeah, what've you got?"

"I'm going to call your cell from this guy's phone. He's been receiving calls from Evana Bahar, instructing him where to go and when to turn on the Electro 451."

"So, it's all been a diversion?" she asked.

"That's what I'm thinking right now. But see if you can trace where those calls have been originating from."

"Can I go now?" the man asked.

Before Hawk could answer, several black SUVs skidded to a stop nearby, and agents poured out. They rushed over to Hawk and Black.

"You're not going anywhere any time soon," Hawk said to the man, turning toward the leader of the team that had just arrived.

"I've been getting updates on the situation developing here," the leader said as he flashed his credentials.

"Look, stick with this guy, and if Evana Bahar directs him to activate his machine again, let him," Hawk said. "I've got everything out of him that I need, but I don't want her to think one of her minions has been compromised. It'll keep the element of surprise on our side."

"You got it. Mind if we inspect the facility before we leave?"

"Be my guest," Hawk said.

He and Black made their way to the car. "Alex, you got anything yet?"

"Just as I feared," she said. "It looks like she's routing all her calls through her phone's browser and has a VPN that's masking her location. The first call looks like it came from Pakistan, while the other one came in from South Africa."

"Well, a lot of good that does us," Hawk said as he got inside.

"At least we can switch up our search," she said.

"Yeah, but we don't even know what to look for now."

"The CIA has recorded that feed," Alex said. "I'm going to analyze the footage and see if I can determine where they were broadcasting from. There might be something in the images that give us a clue as to where they were—or maybe still are."

"Whatever you do, do it in a hurry," Hawk said. "Evana has gone dark, which means she's getting ready for her grand finale with the president."

CHAPTER 24

ALEX LOOKED AT WOOD, who was pacing around the room. She finished the rest of the bottled water he'd given her and stood to stretch. While the night had been full of adrenaline-pumping excitement, she was growing tired of the frenetic pace as well as the number of dead ends.

"How are things going?" Blunt asked.

Alex turned around to see her boss standing there with a faint grin on his face. "You're okay," she said as she gave him a hug.

"And so is Laura," he said, gesturing toward Black's sister.

Alex embraced her. "Are you all right?"

Laura nodded. "I've had enough drama tonight to last me a lifetime."

"You and me both," Alex said.

Wood scowled as he approached the reunion. "Look, not to be a spoilsport here, but we need to let Alex get back to work. We're running out of time to find Evana Bahar before she does something terrible with the president."

"Catch me up to speed," Blunt said. "Maybe I can help."

"As a matter of fact, maybe you can," Alex said.

Wood chuckled. "I didn't know the great J.D. Blunt was also an expert analyst."

"Not to mention a damn fine poker player," Blunt said with a wink.

Alex shook her head. "No, that's not what I'm talking about. I need him to help analyze the footage from the earlier broadcast from Al Fatihin. We need to figure out where they were when they started transmitting. I figure with your extensive knowledge of the city, you might be able to recognize something about the structure of the building where they were or at least see some kind of clue."

"Since Blunt was one of the founding citizens of Washington, I'm sure he'd be an excellent resource for your analysis," Wood said.

"Very funny," Blunt said. "And just to prove your point, I'm going to beat you with my cane when we're finished."

"I'd prefer a poker rematch," Wood said with a wink.

"Come with me," Alex said as she led the group across the room to a bank of monitors. "I set the footage to loop on these large screens. If you see anything that looks familiar, let me know. And I mean anything."

The images rolled on the televisions as everyone stood closely eyeing the broadcast of Evana's torture of President Young. Wood called over several other analysts to ask them if they noticed anything familiar about the room or anything.

"It's so dark; I can hardly see anything," Blunt said.

"Wait a minute," Laura said. "Can you freeze that screen right there and blow up that thing in the back?"

"Sure," Alex said. "Give me a second." She tapped in a few commands on the computer, and the image froze.

"Enlarge this part right here," Laura said, pointing to one corner of the screen.

Alex did as instructed and watched as Laura stared with her mouth agape.

"What is it?" Alex asked.

"I know where that is."

"Where?" Wood asked.

"That's in one of the basement rooms at the Library of Congress," Laura said. "That's the kind of cart we use to transport books around. And it's a genius way to move about the city undetected. You can walk a couple blocks underground, beneath all the buildings that make up the campus."

"How could we have missed this? " Wood asked. "They were right under our noses this whole time. I'm sending another team there now."

"Hawk and Black can meet them at the library."

Wood nodded. "I'll get security to cordon off the area around it, and hopefully we'll trap them there."

Alex turned to Laura. "Do you think you can help us narrow down which room this is?"

"Let me see," she said, resting her chin on the palm of her hand. "Can you lighten up the background so I can tell what color the wall is? We use different color schemes in each of the buildings so employees can readily tell where they are. It's like a maze down there, and you can feel like you're walking forever and forget which way is which."

Alex typed in a few more commands and was able to isolate a portion of the wall behind Young. The color quickly came into focus.

"It's blue," Laura said. "That's the John Adams Building. Now, zoom in on the books."

Alex followed Laura's lead.

"Based on the collection in that cart, I'm going to guess that's the room where we take everything to be re-filed at the end of the day. There are a handful of spaces like this, but it'll be on the west side of the property."

"You're amazing, Laura."

Alex pinged Hawk on the coms. "Are you still out there?"

"Got you loud and clear," Hawk said. "What's cooking?"

"Laura figured out where they were—and hopefully still are," Alex said.

Black smiled as he looked at Hawk. "That's my little sis."

"Where are we headed?" Hawk asked.

"The John Adams Building at the Library of Congress," Alex said. "Look for a room in one of the basements on the west side. Laura is certain that's where they were broadcasting from."

"How did she figure that out?" Black asked.

"She saw one of the book carts in the corner, and we worked together from there to figure it out," Alex said.

"You never could get anything by her," Black said with a chuckle.

* * *

HAWK AND BLACK FLASHED their credentials to the security team assembled around the two blocks that comprised the Library of Congress. Upon entering the John Adams Building, Hawk and Black raced down the steps, coming out in the basement. The main corridor splintered off in four directions.

"According to Alex, we need to look on the west side," Hawk said.

They both scurried toward the area and began their search. With weapons drawn, they moved from room to room, looking for any signs that the Al Fatihin crew had been here.

"Will we know which room exactly?" Hawk asked.

"There's a beige cart loaded with several large books on the Revolutionary War if I'm reading the spine correctly," Alex said. "But other than that, you're on your own."

"Roger that."

After going through a half dozen rooms, they still hadn't found any clue that Al Fatihin was ever here.

"Alex, ask Laura if she's sure," Hawk said.

"She's sure," Black said. "That woman fell in love with this library a long time ago. I'm genuinely surprised she couldn't tell us the exact one given her attention to detail."

Hawk signaled for Black to move with him down the hall.

"She's sure," Alex said. "She also said she thinks it might be the next to the last door on the left of that hallway."

"Well, that's where we're headed next," Hawk said.

Hawk eased the door open and then flicked on the lights. He drew back and waited for any kind of gunfire, but there wasn't even the faintest sound. Black charged ahead, his gun trained forward. In the corner, a few carts were bunched together. Black rushed over to them and started scanning the spines.

"Nothing yet on the Revolutionary War," he said.

"Laura said they are oversized books," Alex said. "That means they're taller than twelve inches high."

Black chuckled.

"What's so funny?" Hawk asked.

"I forgot my tape measure," Black said. "It's so like Laura to know details like that."

"I'm glad you were able to save her tonight, even if you did keep your whole situation a secret from the rest of the team," Hawk said. "Sounds like you two are closer than I realized."

"I don't see her very often anymore due to this line of work, but when we get together, it's like we never were apart. It's a special bond, for sure."

"Hang on," Hawk said. "I think I found it. I'm gonna snap a picture and send it to you Alex. Let me know if this is it."

After Hawk sent the image, he waited for her reply.

"Yep, that's it," she said. "That's the room."

Moments later, CIA agents spilled into the room and fanned out.

"Look for anything that could give us a clue about where they went," Hawk said.

The hunt continued for no more than five minutes before one of the team members shouted at Hawk. "I think I found something."

Hawk and Black hustled over. "I found this book that had a diagram of the Washington Monument that detailed the original design as well as the modern-day improvements. Think that's where they're headed?"

"Did you get that, Alex?" Hawk said.

"Roger that. Wood says all units head to the monument. The FBI will dispatch a couple of SWAT teams as well."

"We're on it," Hawk said.

CHAPTER 25

A'ISHA INSPECTED HER NEW prosthetic leg as she relaxed on a bench near the platform at Union Station. She wanted to remove her leg and never see it again. Playing sports wasn't that important. All she wanted was to be normal and walk without a limp. It's not like anyone ever saw her legs anyway hidden beneath her jilbab. As long as she didn't have a hitch in her gait, she would've been satisfied despite her dreams of playing football with her friends. But this leg came with a price, one so steep she couldn't afford it. She'd become a pawn of Al Fatihin.

A'isha sighed and hung her head, unwilling to absorb the stares she'd felt boring through her from fellow travelers. While she expected to look different than everyone else while visiting the United States for her surgery, she had no idea just how much she would stand out. Everywhere she went, eyes followed her, a mix of curiosity and fear. She could sense some of the people were wondering if she had a suicide vest hidden beneath her cloak.

No, just my dismembered leg from a suicide bomber.

She figured her ability to detect fear so easily stemmed from the fact that she lived under the weight of that same terror each day in Garmsir. And then one day, her worst fear morphed into a sad reality, leaving her with wounds that extended far beyond the ones on her leg. The scars on her heart were the deepest, especially the ones left by her dad. His misguided zeal had left her fatherless and confused. And now her harsh journey had led her to a point where she'd become the weapon.

Agent Nelson patted her on the back as he settled onto the bench next to her. She withdrew from him, sliding a few feet beyond arms' length.

"A'isha, don't be like that," he said in Arabic. "This will all be over soon."

"Will it?" she asked. "I don't even know you."

"I understand," he said. "But right now, I'm the only one who's helping you."

"Is that what you call this?"

"Look, I know it's been tough for you. Your mother was supposed to be here but couldn't make it. Then you get paraded onto the stage during the State of the Union address, unaware that someone had turned your brand new leg into a weapon. Just have a little faith, will you? It's all going to be over with very soon."

"What time does our train get here?" she asked.

"In half an hour or so. Just relax, okay? Nobody knows who you are here."

"But I was on television with the president just a few hours ago."

"Don't worry. Nobody watches live television any more."

No sooner had Agent Nelson uttered those words then a woman passing by stopped in front of them and eyed A'isha closely.

"You're that girl who was on stage tonight with President Young, aren't you?" the woman asked.

"What did she say?" A'isha asked.

Agent Nelson shook his head and rolled his eyes. "What are you, some racist? You see some girl wearing a jilbab like you saw tonight on television and assume that's the same girl? Get a life."

"That's her," she said. "I know it."

"She's an American, and she's my daughter," Nelson said. "And if you don't get the hell outta here, I'm going to report you to security."

The woman bristled as she turned and walked away. After a few steps, she cast a glance over her shoulder back at A'isha.

"I know you're her," the woman said.

"Just ignore her," Nelson said, returning to speaking in Arabic. "People are always afraid of what they don't understand."

A'isha fought back tears as she scooted closer to Agent Nelson. He rubbed her back with his right hand for a moment before a phone call interrupted him.

"Excuse me," he said. "I'll be right back."

She smiled, touched by the genuine warmth she felt from him. As he paced across the platform while speaking on his cell, she watched him intently. His face fell as he glanced at her. When he hung up, he walked back slowly to her.

"What is it?" she asked.

"It's nothing," he said. "You don't have anything to worry about."

"Thank you for helping me," she said.

He nodded and started massaging her neck. That's when she felt a sharp prick.

"Hey," she said. "What was that?"

Everything around her began to get hazy, and after a few seconds, the world went dark as she slumped onto the bench.

CHAPTER 26

PRESIDENT YOUNG REFUSED to comply with the Al Fatihin terrorists who were dragging him toward the Washington Monument. He stumbled forward and remained on the ground until they lifted him to his feet. However, he didn't move until they shoved him forward. He fell again, making the process of getting him to the top more arduous than they'd likely anticipated.

They may have viewed Young as a pushover, but he wasn't going down without a struggle. If they were going to kill him in the Washington Monument, he was going to make sure it was a mess. No neat beheading. No clean execution. He was going to fight them every step of the way.

Evana recoiled before striking him repeatedly in the back and sides with her cropping stick. She knelt next to him, putting her lips just a few inches from his ear.

"Is this a game to you?" she asked. "Because it's not to me. This is very serious. Maybe you think this is fun, just like you do when you send drones to obliterate innocent people in my country, orphaning children and ripping families apart. No, you're going to stand up and take this like a man, though some part of me is certain that you'll be begging for your life like the gutless coward that you are."

She drew back and spit on him before kicking him once more, this time in the face.

Young's whole body ached from the torture. He wasn't sure he had the stamina to do what she asked. Yet he knew it would take more will to deny her the pleasure than it would to get a quick end to his life. He wasn't about to grant her any satisfaction.

"Get up," she said, yanking him up by the back of his collar.

Young staggered to his feet, stumbled forward a few steps, and collapsed again.

"I don't want to shoot you right here, but I will," she said. "Now stand up."

Young moved slowly, partially because he was in so much pain but also because he was hoping that by delaying things that would give someone an opportunity to find him. He groaned as he stood. While he wanted to fall down again and drag out the process, he decided ambling along might be a better approach. As he veered off to the path, Evana laid her shoulder into him, knocking Young back onto the sidewalk.

"I can make this even more painful, you know," she said. "Keep going."

Young plodded along toward the entrance to the Washington Monument. With the recent construction finally completed after several years, he realized Evana's intentions.

Upon reaching the entrance, she swiped an access card in front of the security panel and proceeded to insert a key in the lock. She opened the door and ushered Young inside. But he didn't move.

Instead, Young stood outside and looked toward the top. "I'm not going," he said. "I hate heights."

"Don't worry," Evana said. "You won't be up there for very long."

Young glanced over at Evana and the other Al Fatihin agents following her and made a break down the hill. With the wind in his face, he shouted with joy, even as he realized his final moment of freedom on Earth might be a brief instance of defiance.

The episode ended quickly when two operatives tackled, skinning up his face as he slid along the walkway.

Evana cracked Young several times behind his knees and then again in his ribs. She continued her torture by grabbing him by his hair and jerking a fistful of it up. He rose to his feet and stumbled back toward the entrance.

"You're going up there one way or another," Evana said as she pointed to the top. "Whether you do it consciously or unconsciously is up to you."

Young dipped his shoulder and exploded up, jamming against the guard on his right. Before the other Al Fatihin terrorist on the left knew what was happening, he took a knock to his shoulder.

Young ran a few feet before crumpling and once again falling face first onto the pavement.

"Like I said, Mr. President, you're going up to the top one way or another," she said.

Young felt his cheek sticking to the icy sidewalk. That was the last thing he remembered before Evana kicked him in the head and knocked him out.

CHAPTER 27

HAWK PUMPED HIS ARMS, almost in unison with Black, as they ran toward the Washington Monument. Over the coms, Hawk heard Randy Wood doling out orders to his subordinates and discussing strategy with some other decision makers.

"Alex, let me talk to Wood," Hawk said. "He doesn't know Evana like I do."

"Sure."

After a few seconds, Wood's voice boomed over the coms. "What is it, Hawk?"

"You can't send the cavalry to the Washington Monument."

"This is the President of the United States," Wood said. "We need a decisive response to this brazen attack."

Hawk gasped for breath as he responded. "I understand you're upset, but if you go after her like this, it's probably going to end up with Young getting shot—and I know that's not the goal here."

"Okay, let's suppose for a second that you're in charge," Wood said. "How would you handle this situation?"

"Covertly, quietly, and quickly. If she wants this event streamed so every television station in the world can show the footage of the president getting murdered, then she'll do it. Otherwise, I suggest we keep a low profile."

"How low of a profile are we talking?"

"Let me handle it with Black," Hawk said. "Let us be the ones to approach her."

"Are you telling me you don't think it's a good idea to have a show of force?"

"Not initially. If she senses that it's over, she might end it before we have a chance to save the president. Have them waiting in the wings, and when it's time, you'll know it."

"What's that supposed to mean?" Wood asked.

"Do you remember when Karif Fazil tried to kill Liam Davenport, England's Secretary of State for Defense?"

"How could I forget?"

"Well, I think Evana Bahar is going for a dramatic murder, just like Karif Fazil attempted."

Wood grunted. "It ended well for Davenport, but not for Fazil."

"Exactly," Hawk said. "That's what we're going

for here. But if there had been dozens of sharpshooters surrounding the bridge and ready to take aim on Fazil, he would've likely shot Davenport on the spot to ensure that he exacted revenge. Let's not make a mistake here."

"I understand you're concern, but—"

"Look, you're the one who asked me what to do because I know Evana Bahar better than you do," Hawk said. "And if you want my help, I need you to do what I ask. Send your men, but have them waiting in the wings. We'll get the president back."

Wood sighed. "Fine. I'll make sure my men stay back until you give them the signal. Anything else you want?"

"Yes," Hawk said. "Get me a helicopter at the White House—and a long rope. We're going to need it."

Black shot a glance over at Hawk. "A long rope? Really?"

"I know you hate heights, so I'll do it," Hawk said.

"And let you get all the glory for saving Young's life? Never."

"Trust me. I can handle this."

A couple of minutes later, they reached the Washington Monument. Hawk slowed down as he saw Evana abusing Young, kicking him and prodding him to get to his feet.

"Now what, genius?" Black asked.

"Wait here. I'm going to go talk with her."

Hawk rushed up to the front of the Washington Monument entrance with his weapon trained on the agent jamming his gun into Young's head.

"I suggest you let him go," Hawk said.

Evana Bahar, who was standing a few feet away from Young, steadied her gun on Hawk. "Why do you always have to be so dramatic, Mr. Hawk? You're about to be annihilated, but you're still acting as if you have the ability to change the situation."

"Any situation can be changed," Hawk said. "It's a moment-to-moment thing. But you, on the other hand . . ."

"What about me?" she asked.

"You don't seem interested in changing things for the better."

Evana eyed Hawk carefully. "Perhaps we have different definitions about what a better world is. Have you ever considered that we might have different goals?"

"I think we share a similar goal."

"And what's that?" Evana asked.

"We both want each other dead," Hawk said.

"I can't disagree with that," she said. "And while I'd love to continue this conversation, we really need to get going. And when I say that, what I really mean is that President Young needs to get going."

"You're not going anywhere," Hawk said. "I'm not going to let you take the president through those doors."

Evana laughed. "Try to stop me, and you'll both be dead before you can blink. You didn't think I'd go to all these lengths just to be foiled by you at the very end, did you? You're about to learn just how serious this operation truly is."

Hawk forced a smiled. "More serious than kidnapping the President of the United States and threatening to kill him?"

"It can get far, far more serious," Evana said. "Just ask A'isha what she thought about her time in the U.S."

"What did you do to her?" Hawk asked.

Evana grinned as she looked at her watch. "In exactly twenty minutes from right now, two trains will converge at Union Station, carrying hundreds of people. A'isha is chained to a bench, and if she is moved more than ten feet from where she is, the bomb in her leg will explode—along with the rest of the station. However, if you leave now, I'll send you the code to disarm the bomb once President Young is dead. How's that for changing things for the better?"

"You made this mess to begin with," Hawk said. "You don't exactly deserve sainthood for such a gesture. How do I know you'll uphold your end of the bargain?"

"You don't," she said. "But what other option do you have?"

Hawk took a deep breath. There were always other options, and his mind was whirring to come up with a way to save Young and the people at the train station.

"And if I don't?"

"Don't even think about doing anything else. I've thought of every detail, every possible thing you could do. The communication with the trains is being suppressed by some of my colleagues. And I have someone on site who will tell me if you're not there at the station and will detonate the bomb remotely. The entrance to the monument is also rigged to blow if you try to come after us. So, you have your assignment. I suggest you get going so you can make it in time. If you hurry, you might make it with five minutes to spare."

Hawk walked backward slowly before spinning and racing back to Black, who heard the entire conversation over the coms.

"Sounds like you need to start running to Union Station," Black said.

Hawk shook his head. "No, but you do."

CHAPTER 28

HAWK FELT LIKE HE'D been thrown into a problem that wasn't solvable, a cruel cosmic joke in the most serious of matters. Not only was the life of the president hanging in the balance, but so was the fate of several hundred unsuspecting passengers heading toward Union Station. And while Hawk wasn't confident his plan of action was the best, he knew the eventual outcome if he followed Evana's prescribed steps—and that was also unacceptable. He turned off his coms and told Black to do the same.

"What are we doing?" Black asked.

"Here," Hawk said, removing his hat and jacket. "Wear this, and keep your head down. We look enough alike from a distance. I know that whoever has a finger on that detonator isn't going to be that close by."

They switched clothes as they kept hustling along the path.

"Are you sure this is the right move?" Black asked.

Hawk shook his head. "No, but your training has you better suited than me to disarm a bomb."

"What do you intend to do now?"

"I'm going to save Young. Just keep your coms on, and listen for my command."

Hawk watched as Black launched into a full sprint toward the train station before turning around.

"Alex," Hawk said after turning his coms back on. "Are you still there?"

"I'm here with Blunt and Wood," she said. "You're on speaker too."

"Hawk, this is Randy Wood. I hope you're on your way to Union Station."

"Agent Black is handling that, sir," Hawk said.

Wood grunted. "We can't let all those people die. Noah would never want you to sacrifice all those people for him, especially when it's no guarantee that you can save him."

"We're not sacrificing anyone today," Hawk said. "Were you able to confirm everything Evana said regarding her contingency plan?"

"Yes," Alex said. "We have no way of warning the trains. Someone has taken over the railway servers and is controlling all the communications both on the trains and along the tracks. Short of parking a dump truck at a crossing, we're not stopping anything."

"And what about A'isha? Have you found her yet?"

"She's fastened to a bench near the main platform," Alex said. "There's a tripwire on the lock that's keeping her there."

"Evana truly is evil," Hawk said. "She's weaponized our humanity against us."

"However, we identified the man who took her there, and an FBI team took him down. They're questioning him right now."

Hawk sighed. "By my count, we have seventeen minutes left. It's all going to be too late, especially if I can't figure out a way to get inside the monument."

"There's a secret entrance," a woman blurted out in the back.

"Who said that?" Hawk asked.

"It's me, Laura. During the construction, they didn't want to be seen carting all the supplies and materials into the entrance, so the contractors built a tunnel underneath. I guess now it's like every other building in the city."

"Okay, how do I get to it?"

She explained how Hawk could reach the underground entrance through the nearby visitor's center.

"Hawk, I'm not sure this plan is going to work," Wood said. "There's too much that can go wrong here."

"Sir, I'm afraid everything has already gone all wrong," Hawk said before shooting out the glass to the visitor's center door. He carefully climbed through the glass to get inside. "If we don't try this, we'll all regret it. At least we'll have a chance with this."

"Fine," Wood said. "We'll do it your way. What else do you need?"

"I need a chopper at the White House, ready and waiting to lift off and pick us up on my command."

"I'm not sure we can get something over there that quickly."

"Make it happen," Hawk said. "We only have sixteen minutes left by my count. I'm going up now. Just keep me posted."

Hawk entered the tunnel and sprinted toward the base of the monument. He hustled up to ground level and took a moment to catch his breath. The elevator display showed Evana had already taken Young to the top. After opening the door to the stairwell, Hawk looked upward and shook his head. The steps wound around the massive elevator shaft. He needed to climb five hundred steps, and he'd only have a couple minutes to spare once he reached the viewing deck.

A pair of shots from above echoed throughout the structure.

Hawk drew a deep breath and began his ascent.

* * *

WITH EIGHT MINUTES REMAINING until the two trains were set to converge on Union Station,

Black hustled up to the FBI SWAT members surrounding the entrances. He flashed his badge to one of the men, who waved him inside.

One of the FBI agents rushed over and introduced himself as Agent Reed.

"You looking for the girl?" Reed asked.

Black nodded. "Have you inspected the bomb yet?"

Reed shook his head. "We were instructed to stay away until you arrived."

"Take me to her."

Reed led Black to the platform where A'isha was screaming as she tried to yank her wrist free of the chain that tethered her to the bench.

"You have anyone who can speak Arabic here?" Black said. "We need to get her to calm down."

Reed radioed for someone to come over. "Any onsite agents fluent in Arabic?"

There was no response.

"Anyone?" Reed asked again.

Nothing.

Black crouched down in front of A'isha. "I'm going to help you get your leg off."

She furrowed her brow.

"I'm here to help you," Black said. "Can I lift up your skirt so I can see your leg?"

Black gestured what he wanted A'isha to do. She hesitated at first before slowly tugging up the hem so he could look at her prosthetic limb. After studying it for a few seconds, he shook his head.

"Alex," this is Black. "We've got a problem."

"What now?"

"I don't have time to disarm this bomb, and I can't detach it either."

"That's not surprising given how this is playing out," Alex said. "The man the FBI apprehended who brought A'isha to the train station doesn't have anything on him. He's not the one controlling the detonator."

"Then who is?"

* * *

EVANA BAHAR FORMED a noose with her rope and tugged on it to make sure it was tight. She walked up to the camera that was streaming the public execution of President Young and grinned.

"This is the moment the world has been waiting for," Evana said. "It's time for some of America's leaders to atone for their sins against the rest of the world. All the oppression and imperialism that this nation has perpetrated against everyone else for over two hundred years is going to come crashing down today. Are you ready?"

The Al Fatihin terrorist behind the lens panned over to Young, who was slumped in the corner, blood streaming down his face from another beating Evana had administered upon reaching the top.

Evana stuck her face back in front of the camera. "Too bad he didn't get to finish that stirring speech that was supposed to unite all Americans. Well, what's about to happen is going to bring together all of those citizens of other countries who have been marginalized by America's despotic regimes and tyrannical rule. This is not President Young's world. And he's about to learn that in the most public execution in history."

"It's all lies," Young growled. "She's a liar."

She spun and cracked him in the ribs with her cropping stick.

"Shut up, old man," she said. "Your time is almost up. Your voice will be silenced."

Evana walked behind the camera and stared at the computer. Over five hundred million people were watching the live event.

She measured the rope one more time and tied a knot to secure it on a metal beam she exposed from removing the ceiling tiles.

"On your feet," she said, snatching Young by the back of his collar and yanking him up. "In five minutes, you're going to pay the piper."

* * *

HAWK CONTINUED HIS CLIMB up the stairs and wondered if he'd have any energy left once he reached the top. He could finally see the end and figured he would reach it in less than a minute.

His phone buzzed with a call from a blocked number.

"Yeah," Hawk said.

"I gave you very specific instructions," Evana said. "You were to go to Union Station and wait there until Young was dead. Then I said I'd give you the code to defuse the bomb in the girl's leg."

"And that's what I did," Hawk said.

"What kind of fool do you take me for? Not only are you not there, your FBI friends arrested someone they thought had the detonator. I warned you that I had thought of everything. Now you will all pay a dear price."

"Be careful of switching the game when your opponent has nothing to lose," Hawk said before he hung up on her.

Hawk stopped and raised Alex on the coms.

"So I just heard you struck out with the terrorist you arrested at Union Station," Hawk said.

"How did you—"

"Evana called me to taunt me, which means that she has someone else there who will be activating the bomb remotely, and I know we don't have enough time to isolate whoever that is. Now, has Black made any progress?"

"Negative. He said there's not enough time to disarm it. But what about the Electro 451?"

"I thought about that too, but it won't affect cell towers."

"So now what?"

"I need you to crash all the cell towers in the city so calls can't get through."

"Are you kidding me, Hawk? There's not enough time to do that. And even if I do, that's how law enforcement is communicating with each other. We'd put everyone in the dark."

"Better than everyone dying. Just figure out a way, Alex, and don't tell a soul. If Evana hears about it, she's likely to deviate from her plan again."

"You want me to do this in five minutes?"

"Just do it—and tell Wood to get that chopper airborne. I'm going to need it in about three minutes."

Hawk put his head down and sprinted up the last fifty steps.

CHAPTER 29

HAWK OPENED THE DOOR to the observatory deck and slipped inside. A cool, stiff breeze blew in from where she had already removed the windows. He was hidden from view by the elevator, which was in the center of the room. Just around the corner, he could hear Evana blathering on about how evil the United States was and how she was going to avenge all the terrible things that the American military had done around the world by executing President Young.

Hawk tightened the silencer on the end of his gun. From his vantage point, he couldn't see Evana, but the two other terrorists with her were in the open. Hawk trained his weapon on one of the men before squeezing the trigger. The other man spun in Hawk's direction, opening up and exposing his chest to Hawk. One shot to the center mass and one bullet to the head and the man crumpled to the floor.

Peeking around the edge, Hawk darted back when Evana fired in his direction.

"Face it, Mr. Hawk. It's over. Your beloved president is going to die, and there's nothing you can do about it."

Hawk leaned against the wall and pondered his next move. "Well, he's not dying the way you want him to."

He blasted the camera, which toppled over with a clatter.

"Nobody's going to see what happens now," Hawk said. "It's just you and me."

"I should put a bullet in his head right now," she said.

"But you won't," Hawk said. "You want to prove that you were better than Karif Fazil. You wanted a grander execution, a larger moment to solidify your legacy as a terrorist leader."

"I'm not a terrorist," she said. "I'm a freedom fighter, warring against your nation's tyranny."

"Call yourself whatever you wish, but it doesn't change the reality of who you are."

"Make another step toward me and I'm putting a bullet in Young's head and tossing his body out of the window."

"And then what? You're a martyr for your cause? If that was really what you were after, you would've strapped a vest to your chest a long time ago. No, you don't want to die."

Hawk peeked around the corner, and a bullet ricocheted off the wall near him. He couldn't see or hear what she was doing.

"It's all over if you try anything. I'll shoot Young, and if my man at Union Station doesn't hear from me in three minutes, he's been instructed to detonate the bomb once those trains arrive in the terminal. So you want to reconsider your approach right now if you want to save all those innocent Americans. Now, lay down your weapon and I'll make the call. Young still dies, but at least all those people don't."

"I can't do that," he said.

"It's your choice. All that blood will be on your hands. Is that what you really want?"

Hawk took a deep breath and crouched. He slid his gun across the floor and out into the open so Evana could see it while he remained hidden around the corner.

"There, I did it," Hawk said. "Now make the call."

After a few tense seconds, her phone slammed against the back wall near Hawk, splintering into hundreds of pieces.

"Looks like it's not your day, Mr. Hawk. I can't get a signal. Goodbye."

Hawk peered around the edge in time to see her fling Young over the side and jump after him. Rushing to the opening, Hawk watched as dozens of canisters on the ground spewed a thick smoke into the air, and Evana disappeared from sight.

Just below him, Young kicked and twisted, grasping at the rope around his neck trying to avoid suffocating. Hawk shimmied down the rope.

"I need that chopper over here now with a harness on the end," Hawk said over the coms as he slid down next to Young. He struggled for a few more seconds before passing out.

Clinging to the rope with one arm, Hawk hoisted Young up the wall and pinned him there with a knee. Hawk could hear the helicopter churning toward them as he struggled to keep Young from dropping.

"What's happening?" Young asked as he slowly regained consciousness.

"Just stay still, sir," Hawk said. "No sudden movements. I've got you."

Young tilted his head down and screamed. "No, no," he said. "This is not how I want to die."

"You'll kill the both of us if you don't stay still. Now, please, sir, remain calm."

Hawk's arm was burning as he felt his hand starting slip down the rope. He wasn't sure how much longer he could hold on.

* * *

AT LANGLEY, Alex removed her earpiece from the

coms and asked someone else to monitor it for her. She hammered the keys at her terminal.

"How are we looking?" Blunt asked.

"I'm almost there."

"So is that train. Please hurry."

Alex glanced at the countdown she'd started. She knew she wasn't going to make it.

"Tell Black to do something to keep those trains from reaching the terminal."

"What can he do?"

"Tell him to get creative."

* * *

BLACK RECEIVED THE MESSAGE from Alex over the coms that she needed him to buy her more time to keep the cell towers down. He thought for a moment what might actually work since they had no way of communicating with anyone on the train.

"What if the bomb had already exploded?" he wondered aloud.

Any competent engineer wouldn't keep chugging into the station. He'd slam on the brakes and do everything to keep from tearing into a dangerous situation.

Black ran to a nearby bar and found several FBI agents he knew. "I need your help right now."

"What are we doing?" one of the men asked.

"We're going to make Molotov cocktails."

They worked quickly to make a half dozen bombs to toss into the tunnel.

"The trains are going to be arriving in one minute," Blunt said. "Whatever you're doing, you better hurry."

Black and one of the agents dashed down one tunnel, while the other two men took over in the opposite direction. After sprinting fifty yards deep, Black lit the cloth hanging out of the top and hurled it down the tracks, repeating the process until all three had turned into a roaring blaze.

Black sprinted back to the platform and strained to hear. After a few tense seconds, the sound of screeching brakes reverberated down the tunnel. Seconds later, he heard the same sound from the other direction as well.

"It's done," Black said.

"Almost there," Alex said. "Just need two more minutes."

Black sprinted back toward the flames to explain the situation to the engineer. After a couple of minutes, Alex was back on the coms with the good news.

"Check your phones," she said.

"I've got nothing," Black said.

He hustled back to the platform where A'isha was. She was curled up in a fetal position, sobbing quietly.

"It's over," he said. "I'm going to diffuse this bomb now."

* * *

HAWK CLUNG TO THE ROPE and wondered if he could hold onto it and Young for more than another minute or so. If Hawk let go of Young, he would be dead very soon.

"Where's that chopper?" Hawk asked.

"Look above you," Wood said.

Hawk glanced up and saw two Marines descending out of a helicopter toward him, each holding a harness. The first soldier placed a harness on Young before slashing him free from the rope that secured him to the monument. Once that soldier was finished, the other one steadied Hawk before they were reeled upward. They were all reeled into the aircraft before it peeled away toward the hospital.

"Thanks," Hawk said over the coms. "Mr. Deputy Director, the president is safe and is going to make it."

"The whole nation needs to be thanking you, Hawk," Wood said. "That was incredible. I thought the president was gone for good."

"How are things at Union Station?" Hawk asked.

"They're great," Alex said. "Black just finished diffusing the bomb and is getting A'isha back to the hospital. She's pretty shaken up as you can imagine, but she's alive—and so is everyone else."

"I knew you could do it, honey," Hawk said.

"Well, I did need Black to buy me some extra time and keep the trains out of the station, but it was enough to get the job done."

"Teamwork makes the dream work," Hawk said with a chuckle. "Now, what about Evana Bahar? Any sign of her?"

"We're still searching," Wood said. "But so far, nothing."

"We'll find her, sir. Don't worry. She's got a lot to answer for."

CHAPTER 30

TWO DAYS LATER, the Phoenix Foundation team reconvened at a CIA safe house just outside the capital to discuss how to move forward. Blunt lumbered to the head of the table, a cigar hanging out of his mouth. He flung a stack of file folders in front of the rest of his operatives.

"Well, that was one helluva night," Blunt said. "The president told me he'd give you all commendation medals in a public ceremony except for that fact that this little outfit doesn't really exist."

"And we'd like to keep it that way," Hawk said.

"Has anyone figured out how this all went down?" Alex asked. "This had to be meticulously planned."

Blunt nodded. "It was—and it's obvious that Evana Bahar did a masterful job of predicting what we would do every step of the way."

"Until the very end," Hawk said. "She was definitely counting on me to head to Union Station."

"That was the closest of calls," Blunt said, "but we did what we could to help Alex."

"The thing I can't get over is that Evana had to have some help on the inside," Hawk said. "We already know that Obsidian was working with her."

"Yeah," Black said. "They wanted me to assassinate the Vice President. The only reason they'd do that is because they have the Speaker of the House in their back pocket."

Hawk nodded. "Charlie Knox, the longtime representative from California. He seems like an odd choice."

Blunt grunted. "I think we know by now that Obsidian can reach anyone of any political persuasion as long they apply enough pressure."

"Uh, guys," Alex said as she scrolled through her phone. "I'm not sure Charlie Knox was their man. He died last night of a heart attack, exactly one month after getting a clean bill of health from his doctor."

"Then who's next?" Black asked. "The president pro tempore of the senate?"

"Richard Joseph from Virginia. He's serving his third term now after being a two-term governor."

"Black, I want you to look into Joseph and see what you can find," Blunt said. "We need be watching him closely but from under the radar. I don't trust anyone anymore, not even Randy Wood."

"Admit it—you cheated while playing him in poker, didn't you?" Alex asked. "I always heard you can tell a lot about a man's character by how he plays cards."

"I didn't cheat," Blunt said. "I beat him fair and square. He's just pissed he lost. He'll get over it."

"Well, I guess we'll find out tonight," Alex said. "Because you're all coming over to our place to grill some steaks and play cards."

"Is that really necessary?" Blunt asked. "I'd rather just sit at home tonight and read a book."

"You're coming over, and I won't take no for an answer."

Blunt sighed. "In that case, I'll be there."

"Now switching subjects again—what about A'isha?" Alex asked. "What's happened to her?"

"She's still in the hospital for more observation on her leg," Blunt said. "When she gets out, we'd like to send her back to Afghanistan, but we might as well be sending that girl to her death if we do that. I suspect someone will be watching out for her and making sure she gets in a great home and a good education."

Hawk shook his head. "Everybody gets their happy ending but me."

"You're still married to the hottest operative in the world, and you saved the president," Alex said.

"What's sad about that?"

"Evana Bahar is still out there," Hawk said. "And she's going to be terrorizing innocent people soon enough, if not killing dozens upon dozens of them for her misguided cause."

"We're going to catch her, Hawk," Blunt said. "Just be patient. Remember how long it took us to catch Karif Fazil?"

"I'll never forget it."

Blunt nodded. "Well, we haven't been at this nearly as long, and she only narrowly escaped after her attempt on Young's life. She'll make another mistake at some point, and you'll be right there to nab her."

"Maybe, but it seems like we went through a whole helluva lot of trouble to boost the president's flagging ratings. It's well above fifty percent now for the first time since just days after he was sworn in."

"What's he up to?" Hawk asked.

"Eighty percent," Blunt said.

"Those are sympathy numbers. Once he gets back to the business of governing this country, those polls will drop again. If not on their own, they'll fall because President Young does something that defies logic and makes people uneasy."

Blunt shrugged. "Who cares? Our job is to keep this country safe. And if they somehow coincide with the president's wishes, so be it. We'll reap the benefits as we fulfill our duty."

"So, what's next?" Black asked.

"I hope you'll like this answer," Blunt said.

"Try me," Black said.

"We're getting back to Obsidian being our main focus," Blunt said. "You all think you can handle that?"

Every head bobbed with a yes.

"Very well then," Blunt said. "Let's launch an investigation into Richard Joseph—and find General Fortner so we can put this whole issue to rest. Meeting adjourned."

Blunt stood and lingered for a moment before asking Hawk to stay behind. Once the room was clear, Blunt sat back down.

"What is it, sir?" Hawk asked.

"I need your help. I have a lead for a person connected to Obsidian—and I don't want the team finding out about it. Think you can do that for me?"

Hawk nodded as Blunt slipped his top agent a sheet of paper. He scanned the document for a few seconds as his eyes widened.

"Are you sure about this?" Hawk asked.

Blunt nodded. "I'm sure of the source but not of the accusation. That's why I need you to check it out for me."

"Of course, sir. You can count on me."

THE END

ACKNOWLEDGMENTS

I am grateful to so many people who have helped with the creation of this project and the entire Brady Hawk series.

Krystal Wade was a big help in editing this book as always.

I would also like to thank my advance reader team for all their input in improving this book along with all the other readers who have enthusiastically embraced the story of Brady Hawk. Stay tuned ... there's more Brady Hawk coming soon.

ABOUT THE AUTHOR

R.J. PATTERSON is an award-winning writer living in southeastern Idaho. He first began his illustrious writing career as a sports journalist, recording his exploits on the soccer fields in England as a young boy. Then when his father told him that people would pay him to watch sports if he would write about what he saw, he went all in. He landed his first writing job at age 15 as a sports writer for a daily newspaper in Orangeburg, S.C. He later attended earned a degree in newspaper journalism from the University of Georgia, where he took a job covering high school sports for the award-winning *Athens Banner-Herald* and *Daily News*.

He later became the sports editor of *The Valdosta Daily Times* before working in the magazine world as an editor and freelance journalist. He has won numerous writing awards, including a national award for his investigative reporting on a sordid tale surrounding an NCAA investigation over the University of Georgia football program.

R.J. enjoys the great outdoors of the Northwest while living there with his wife and four children. He still follows sports closely. He also loves connecting with readers and would love to hear from you. To stay updated about future projects, connect with him over Facebook or on the inter-webs at www.RJPbooks.com and sign up for his newsletter to get deals and updates.

Printed in Great Britain
by Amazon